the window

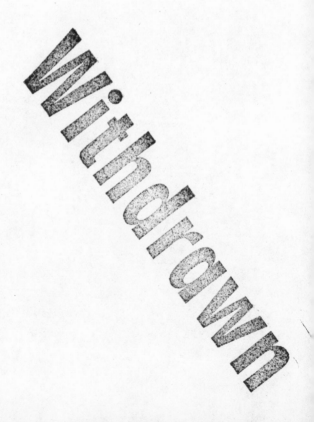

jeanette ingold

the window

harcourt brace & company

san diego   new york   london

Library of Congress Cataloging-in-Publication Data
Ingold, Jeanette.
The window/by Jeanette Ingold.
p.   cm.
When she comes to live with relatives on a Texas farm,
fifteen-year-old Mandy encounters the grandmother she never
knew and begins to come to terms with her blindness caused
by the automobile accident that killed her mother.
ISBN 0-15-201265-6   ISBN 0-15-201264-8 (pbk.)
[1. Mothers and daughters—Fiction. 2. Blind—Fiction.
3. Physically handicapped—Fiction. 4. Family life—Fiction.
5. Ghosts—Fiction.] I. Title.
PZ7.I533Win   1996
[Fic]—dc20   96-1293

Text set in Fairfield Medium
Designed by Camilla Filancia
First edition   A B C D E F   A B C D E F (pbk.)

Printed in Hong Kong

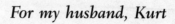

For my husband, Kurt

a c k n o w l e d g m e n t s

I wish to acknowledge with gratitude the
assistance of the teachers and counselors
who answered my numerous questions and
who read and commented on the manuscript:
Fred Bischoff, Judy O'Toole-Freel, Bob Maffit,
Dennis Slonaker, and Dr. Karen Wolffe;
of willing readers Jamie and Kristy Maffit;
of students at the Montana School for the
Deaf and the Blind who reviewed the
manuscript and talked about it with me;
and of my good friends who gave varied
and valued help: Peggy Christian, Hanneke
Ippisch, Wendy Norgaard, Dorothy Hinshaw
Patent, Greg Patent, and Carol Soth.
I especially thank my editor, Diane D'Andrade.

the window

$$\begin{array}{c}) \;) \\ ) \\ ) \;) \end{array}$$

S TAY SEATED, Mandy," the flight attendant says. "When the other passengers have gotten off, I'll come get you."

Right. She should try staying seated herself, when everybody else is standing up and the guy by the window wants out and stuff's tumbling from the overhead bins and you get bumped half into the aisle.

A man says, "Watch it," and some other man says, "Hey." Suddenly there's a pocket of hot silence. Everyone around has just realized I can't see.

"Those must be your folks. They've got a sign with MANDY on it."

Then a woman is hugging me, Aunt Emma I guess. Her front is soft and she's shorter than me. She laughs, flustered. "I knew you were fifteen, but somehow I hadn't pictured . . . I mean, I thought of you younger . . ."

A man hugs me, and another, hugs of wool jackets and aftershave, clumsy big hugs, and their voices rumble.

One tells me he's my uncle Gabriel. Great-uncle Gabriel. They're all greats, for that matter, Great-uncles Abe and Gabriel and Great-aunt Emma, who is Gabriel's wife.

"So, Mandy," he says, "I hope you're going to liven up our gloomy old house."

"Gabriel, hush," Aunt Emma whispers. "It's too soon."

"Don't worry about me," I say. "It's OK."

And even if it's not, I can take care of myself.

That's my gift. Other girls get blond hair and nice families and brains that tell them the right things to say. I've got knowing how to take care of myself, and how to face what I have to face.

Like that night I woke up in the hospital

and heard the nurses talking about whether they should take me to my mom. One said, "I hate for her to see," as if there was any way I could through bandages over eyes that had stopped working.

Besides, did that nurse think I couldn't imagine how my mom was? That I couldn't guess what happened to people when they got thrown from cars and smashed against utility poles?

I fussed until she put me into a wheel-chair, took me to another floor, to intensive care, and I was too dumb to wonder why I was getting to go there now when they hadn't let me for days and days.

"Here's your mother," the nurse told me, and I had to take her word for it. The only sounds in the room were machine sounds.

I found my mother's arm, reached for her face, but the nurse moved my hand away. "You'll dislodge the tubing."

I listened for Mom to make some noise, even to just breathe out loud, but all the room became one steady, tiny monitor blip.

"Hey, Mom," I said, "you sure we can afford the rent here?"

I could feel the nurse get uptight, knew

she was thinking: Hard case; people like these don't have feelings like they should.

"Don't worry, Mom," I said. "I'll get along."

My mom died the next morning, without me ever knowing if she'd heard.

This is my first time to Texas. The cold air surprises me. Somehow I thought Texas, even in the north, would be warm and dusty-smelling, not damp and cold and made empty by a wind without scent. There is no sun; I would feel it through my eyelids. I would see it. I can see sunlight, bright light. There is none this day.

We drive a long while after leaving the Dallas airport, first over highway and then back roads, and then I'm inside a house and still chilly. Aunt Emma puts a bundlely sweater on my shoulders and I hear a furnace come roaring on. "Cold November," says Uncle Abe. "We'll have heat in just a few minutes."

I can't stop a shiver.

"Em," says Abe, "guess we've got another cold-blooded one," and I think he's saying that I'm mean, but he's not.

Gabriel says, "Your Uncle Abe means thin-blooded. Emma always wants the heat up."

The house smells of cooking, onion and broccoli and meats layered one meal into the next, nice smells, but smells.

And of flowers, but not sweet ones like my roommate's at the hospital. I ask Aunt Emma what kind and she says marigolds. "About the last, I guess. We could get frost any night now."

"Most people plant marigolds to keep deer away," says Gabriel, "that's how bad they smell. But Em likes them."

"An honest smell," says Aunt Emma, "and they're easy to grow." Her answer starts another question. It seems to hang in the air: This Mandy, does she grow easy?

No, I want to shout. I don't grow easy. I'm trying the best I can and messing up terribly and I don't see how the three of you are going to make anything any better.

No, I want to shout. Don't you read? It's never easy to raise a child, not even for the people whose job it's supposed to be. Mothers grow children. Not great-aunts and old uncles.

No, I want to shout. Stare at me, in this

bundlely sweater. I don't even know quite where to look, now that you're silent and your voices don't tell me where you are. Do I look easy to grow?

"May I see my room, please?" I ask.

Again that silence. I'd said, *May I see.* You'd think I'd know better, would have learned these last weeks what *see* and *look* do to people who can, when they hear the words said in front of someone who can't. When someone who can't says them herself.

"Certainly," answers Aunt Emma. She laughs, an embarrassed little laugh. "Actually, we have a choice for you. About what room you want, I mean. There's one here on this floor . . ."

"Aren't your bedrooms all upstairs?"

I know they are. Mom had a picture of this house, though she'd never been in it. "My mother's house," she'd say, when she'd find me looking at it. "Your grandmother's."

Again that embarrassed little laugh. "Yes," Aunt Emma says, "but there's a little room down here, a study, that we thought you could . . ."

"Whose study?"

6

"Well, your uncle Abe's, but . . ."

"I don't need it," he breaks in. "I can work perfectly well upstairs. Lots of space in my bedroom for a desk."

I ask, "What's the other choice?" I know what they're doing, trying to give me a room where I won't have to climb steps. But I'm blind, not crippled.

"The other one is on the second floor," says Emma, "but it's so tiny . . ."

It's Uncle Gabriel who interrupts this time. "Actually, there's another choice," he says. "Nobody's using the attic room, nobody has for years. It's not much bigger, but . . ."

"Let me see it, please."

I am not going to stop saying *see* just to spare their feelings. It's what I mean. And what do they want me to say, anyway? *Let me feel the attic, please? Smell the attic?* Choose it for my bedroom without learning one thing about it first?

It's Gabriel who puts my hand on his arm and walks me to the staircase. I run the tip of my long cane side to side. The bare treads are wood and very wide, worn to rounded edges.

"It's a long flight," he says.

I start up on my own, as rapidly as I can go and not hesitating once, even when I'm thinking, Please God help me find the top so I take a smooth step onto it and don't fall on my face. And I do it right.

I wait for the others. Aunt Emma comes up wheezing. I've made her climb the steps faster than she usually does. Abe doesn't come up at all.

"The attic?" I ask. "How do we get there?"

I start to unpack by myself, opening my suitcase on a high, creaking bed. It's afternoon now, and someone has cleaned and made the bed with sheets and a puffy quilt. Aunt Emma comes in long enough to hang lace curtains. "Washed and pressed," she says. "They don't give much privacy, but there's no one out there but cows."

She chatters as she works, telling me about Herefords and Angus and how the uncles are thinking of trying some exotic breed.

I hear metal snap. "There, done," Aunt Emma says. An instant later she touches my

8

hand. "Mandy," she begins. "Mandy, I'm glad your caseworker found us. Your uncles and I had no idea we even had a niece."

I can't decide which response to pick from the several that come to me: I'm not your niece, I'm your grandniece; I didn't know about you, either; I must have been some surprise. Any one of them would lead to more talk, when all I want is to be left alone.

"If you don't mind," I say, "I'll finish unpacking now."

I find the closet and a dresser and put away my clothes, becoming angry all over again about how much is missing. Half my things got thrown away by the child services woman who closed up the apartment after Mom died, I guess because she thought my stuff looked cheap. "It wasn't your right," I told her when I learned what she'd done. She'd answered, "Your needs will be different in Texas."

At least she left me my photos. Now I stand them on a dressing table. Mom. Her dad, who died before she was born. I touch the glass in the frames.

The sun has come out now and it's

making the attic too warm. I go toward the sun, feel behind the curtains to the window latch, unlock and raise the window. Fresh, cold air rushes in, blowing the curtains against my face. I hold them aside and lean out, into the wind. There's someone calling.

I lean out farther, to hear. . . .

"Gwen. GWEN. Where are you?"
It was a child's voice. "GWEN?"

Footsteps sound on the stairs. "Mandy," Aunt Emma is saying, "I've got towels . . . Oh, child, be careful. Don't lean so far out."

"I heard something," I tell her. "Who is that boy calling? Wanting Gwen?"

There's a space before she answers. Too long a space. "There's no one out there, child. You must be hearing the curtains whisper."

chapter 2

I LEARN QUICKLY that this is a house of routine, with times for everything. If a time needs to be changed, nobody makes a big deal, but everyone knows. Something's changed.

Enter Mandy. They must hate how I'm making everything in their lives change.

Like Tuesday morning, my first morning in this house. Breakfast here is a sit-down, all-together affair that starts at 7:15. Tuesday I make the start but I'm late for the finish. One minute there's forks clinking against plates and talk about hay and pregnant cows and shopping lists, and the next minute I'm the only one left eating.

"Don't wait for me," I say, but they do, and I know they're all replanning their mornings because I'm making things slow, have made them change what they do.

A wave of longing for my mom, and for the easy way we lived, washes over me. Mom and I, we never had anything set enough *to* change.

"Hungry, babe?" she'd ask, whenever she thought about food. It might be five in the afternoon or nine at night. Or 3:00 A.M., when she'd been awake and I'd heard her prowling in the hall. She'd know I wasn't sleeping, either, and ask, "Hungry, babe?"

The memory is so strong I can hear her voice, and Gabriel's voice cutting through it is a jolt.

"If you're done, Mandy," he says, "let's give Emma a hand with the dishes."

"I don't think Mandy should . . . ," Emma begins.

But Gabriel's saying, "The door's just behind you, Mandy."

He doesn't leave me any choice but to start toward it, even as I'm thinking, No, I can't help and I shouldn't be in a kitchen and please, how will I keep from breaking things and what if the stove's still on?

Emma must be thinking the same things, because as soon as I step from carpet to tile, she's by my side. "Mandy, I'll walk you to the sink," she says.

I let her guide me, and, reassured I won't get hurt, I move forward until I brush against something off to the right. "The kitchen table, Mandy," Emma says. "The refrigerator is along the wall to your left."

I reach out and find its smooth, cool front.

"Next there's more counter," Emma says, and I'm going to touch that, too, but before I can her voice sharpens into a warning. "Don't, there's the stove next."

I jerk my hand back and right away hope no one has seen me do it. I will not let on that this scares me; I will not.

And tumbling after that thought is the realization I'd jerked my hand away from warmth.

As we round a corner I say what I've just learned, say it as though it's something I've known all along: "You don't have to worry about me getting burned. I'd feel heat before I'd actually touch a burner."

But I'm thankful to hear Emma say, "That's enough exploring. Why don't you stand here?"

Then someone's handing me a towel and soon I'm drying pots and lids, laying them on the counter. For a bit there's the *whish* and soft clang of Aunt Emma working at the sink and the clatter of the uncles loading things into the dishwasher. Then Emma says, "Mandy, we need to talk about what's next for you."

One of the uncles takes a frying pan from my hand.

"We're asking, Mandy," says Gabriel. "What do you want to do?"

The question is school. Where. If I want to go away to this special one where there would be other blind kids or if I want to try the high school in town.

Already my child study team has met with my aunt and uncles to go over reports from the rehab center where I was before coming here. I guess they've all pretty much decided the final decision can be left up to me. "She has potential for success in either environment" was the way it was put.

The special school, which I'd have to board at, would have more equipment and a lot of specialists to teach me all the things I suddenly need to know. And—get this bit—my "chances of social integration would be greatly enhanced."

The local high school has some stuff, too, mainly in a resource room, but I'd be expected to do most of my work in regular classes. I could count on some help from itinerant teachers, teachers who go from school to school to work with kids like me, but, for sure, I'd be a lot more on my own.

Now Uncle Gabriel breaks into my thoughts. "So, time for a command decision," he says. "Pros and cons either way."

He doesn't have to spell out the cons, and, besides, I doubt if he thinks of the same ones I do. A school of fifteen hundred normal kids—will they make room for me? Whisper and watch me? Will they laugh at me?

Don't be stupid, Mandy, I think. Of course they will, but since when haven't you been able to handle being the outsider?

Mandy the new girl, I think. Mandy the new blind girl. So what's the difference?

I don't fool myself. The difference is huge and lies, cold and sick-feeling, in the pit of my stomach. I swallow back welling saliva.

"The town school, I guess," I say.

It's not a guess, though. More a gamble, or a chance I have to take. I'm afraid *not* to try, afraid to disappear into that special school for blind kids. I'm not ready to give up, to disappear from my life. I don't ever want to be.

"The regular high school," I repeat.

There's a trick to first days, days when you're the new girl and you've got to let everyone know where you'll fit into things. Blow it, and you might as well quit trying, because nobody's going to give you another chance.

I'd had it down, always wore my good-luck T-shirt and amber skirt, my hair in a single braid pinned up like I took ballet or ran track. I'd pause at the classroom doorway, flash a confident smile, make eye contact with the kids who looked like they ran things. I wanted them to know I was there.

Of course, I'd had a lot of practice with first days. Mom and I were forever moving ahead of a rent check coming due. Or behind Mom losing her job. Or with some story Mom had read about how life's better in West Virginia, or cheaper in Arizona because you don't have heating bills, or healthier in the mountains or on the desert or by the ocean.

Over the years Mom and I moved south to get religion, north to get away from it, west to escape from some creep who stalked Mom the time we tried Philadelphia.

Yeah, I've had a lot of practice with first days.

Except I've never done one blind before. And I don't have my amber skirt. It's gone, along with all the other clothes the child services woman didn't approve of.

That evening I ask, "Aunt Emma?"

"Yes, Mandy?"

"Do I have any money?"

"Money!"

"Well, left from my mother. Insurance . . . ?"

"Don't worry about it. We've got enough."

"I mean, my own money. That I can spend how I want."

I guess the answer's no, although Emma doesn't exactly say that, but later on Uncle Gabriel gives me some folded bills. "I hear you need an allowance," he says. "Why don't you plan on fifteen dollars a week?"

"You're just giving it to me?" I ask. "What do you expect me to do with it?"

I don't mean to be rude, but I know from Gabriel's answer that's how I've sounded.

"I expect, Mandy, that you'll use it to buy what you need, that you'll save some, that you'll pay your way when you do things with friends." His voice lightens up. "Pitch in gas money, maybe, if you go somewhere."

Is this man for real? What friends does he imagine?

I want to tell Uncle Gabriel I don't need his allowance, but I keep my mouth shut. A person doesn't turn down money.

Two days later we all drive to town so I can get some clothes to start school in.

The uncles drop Aunt Emma and me off at the department store end of a mall, saying they're going to check on some motor repairs and will pick us up when we're done. "What do you want?" Gabriel asks. "Half an hour or so?"

"A couple of hours at least," Aunt Emma says. "And bring the checkbook back. Why don't you meet us about noon in the coat department?"

She's laughing as we go in. "Half an hour! Isn't that just like a man, Mandy?"

She steers me across an echoing, perfume-smelling place and into an elevator, where a woman greets her by name.

"Anne, this is my grandniece, Mandy," Emma says.

I don't have any idea if I'm being introduced to a clerk or a friend or what. I say hi and someplace inside hear the voices of a dozen teachers saying, "Speak up, Mandy."

I expect Emma to say, "Speak up, Mandy," but she doesn't. Instead, she tells how we're going to the junior department. She makes it sound like the most exciting thing she's ever done.

Then we're getting out of the elevator, which hasn't stopped quite flush with the floor. I stumble, and this woman, Anne, grabs my arm. She says, "Let me help," and she's pulling me forward before I can get my bearings again. When I try to shake off her hand, she grips me harder.

"I don't need your help," I say. "Let me go." I can hear that I'm too loud.

There's a moment of embarrassed silence, a tiny "Well . . ." from the woman, not angry exactly but uncertain. Then she's saying good-bye, and good shopping, and telling Emma she'll talk to her later. I bet.

I expect Emma to scold me for being rude, but she just says, "This way."

We seem to be the only ones shopping in juniors, I suppose because it's a school morning. Aunt Emma asks what kind of things I like, but I've hardly started to tell her when a clerk comes up and takes over.

"This is my niece," Aunt Emma says, "my grandniece," like it matters who I am. "We're here for school clothes."

"What size is she?" asks the clerk.

"I'm an eight," I say.

"Does she like pants or skirts?"

"Ask me," I say. "I'm the one who will wear them."

And then, to my horror, tears well up.

"Want to get a cola and try this later?" Aunt Emma asks.

"No," I say, "now."

"Look," says the clerk, "I'm sorry, I didn't mean . . ." and then Aunt Emma's smoothing things over and pretty soon I'm in a dressing room.

I stand there while the clerk brings in things and holds them up to me. She says, "See how this fits," or "Navy's not your color."

There's so much I want to know. . . . I mean, clothes matter. I feel the tops of collars, try to picture how a neckline is. Where a hem is hitting my legs. Everything seems long, and I say so.

"I can call in the seamstress, but of course that's an extra charge," says the clerk.

"We can take them up at home," Aunt Emma says.

I'm happiest with the jeans—jeans fit or they don't, and you don't need eyes to tell. And with one blouse, the material feels like air between my fingers and I hear Aunt Emma catch her breath when she sees it on me. Or maybe she's gasping at the price tag. Nobody talks about what anything costs, but the blouse feels expensive.

Shopping does take until noon, between the junior department and shoes. I'm picking out a jacket when my uncles arrive.

Uncle Gabriel pays for it all, and I wonder if I should offer to give back the money he gave me, but I can't find a moment when it feels right to ask. This is the first time in my life I have bought more than one thing at a time.

Emma and the uncles are ready to go out to lunch, but suddenly I'm so tired I can hardly stand up. "Please," I say, "can we go home?"

The next thing I know, Emma is shaking my shoulder and Abe is saying, "We're here, Mandy."

It takes all of us to carry everything up to my room. We pile it on my bed, and Aunt Emma says she'll help me take off tags and hang stuff up.

"No," I say, "I'll do it, if you'll tell me where to find scissors."

I can feel Emma's disappointment. A twinge of guilt shoots through me, but I can't take more help, not today.

Alone, I empty a sack, find underwear. I start with a pair of underpants, spread them flat, and run my hand all over one side, all

04978 5574

over the other, inside the waistband. Only one tag, pinned in, and I take that off.

Emma comes back up and puts something metal in my hand. She's gone again before I identify the nail clippers she's given me instead of scissors.

The skirt and jeans and tops, they're harder to deal with than the pants were. The price tags are all attached by those stiff plastic strings, the kind that end in *T*s. The clippers work on most, but there's one tag that's caught in a seam and I finally give it a yank that makes something tear.

I'm doing the last pair of jeans when I stab my finger on a pin. I suck a bit of blood and wait and wait, lick my finger clean and wait some more. What if I get blood on my new clothes and don't know?

And then I put it all away, the underwear folded in a dresser drawer, the other things on hangers. The clothes feel right, but I wish I could see them, could be sure they're OK.

I wish I knew what sort of Mandy the kids are going to see.

I've got the window open because the attic was stuffy when we got back from shopping. Now cold wind hits me and I go over to close it.

The curtains billow up, and I duck under.

I reach for the window, again hear a child's thin voice calling.

I lean out.

"Gwen, Gwen, GWEN."

"Who's down there?" I call.

"Gwen, where are you?"

The boy sounds closer now, and I lean out farther.

Wind gusts and the next instant a curtain panel blows around me. For an instant I imagine I'm in the hospital again, waking up inside bandages. Then the house smells bring me back, bleach and dust from the windowsill.

My fingers scrabble with the curtain, searching for the edges.

And then I hear my own voice but not mine, my voice with somebody else's accent. . . .

"Abe, go away," the voice says.

chapter 3

THE WIND GUSTS again, and I'm moving with it, spiraling from November to summer, from dark to light, tumbling until I'm really seeing, watching another girl. She hangs by her knees from a tree limb, one hand holding up her skirt, the other dragging in the dirt. She looks about my age.

A little boy is with her, in the shade under the big tree, and I can hear him talking. . . .

"Gwen, you better come down out of that tree. Mama's looking for you everywhere."

"Go away, Abe."

"Mama will get you, Gwen. You know she

said you're too big to be climbing trees. I can see your underpants."

"And you're too little to matter." Gwen pulled herself up, then dropped back to hang from her knees so fast that bark scraped her legs and the little boy sucked in his breath. "Tell Mama I'll be along in a bit."

She stretched down both hands and dragged the tips of her fingers in the summer dust.

I stand back from the window, touch its frame.

What has happened?

My question is smothered in an answer that wells up, scary and impossible and, especially, exciting. Can I have seen into another time?

Mandy, I tell myself, you're losing it. Imagination plus.

But the sharp detail of leg and cotton dress is bright inside my eyelids, and the Texas accents echo in my ears. They're so real, and that moment of being able to see again so clear in my mind, that I feel disoriented.

I go to the closet and find my new clothes. Count the four pair of jeans.

Go to the door.

"Uncle Abe?" I call.

"Yes?" he calls back, his voice full and deep and ragged, a grown man's voice. "You need something, Mandy?"

"No," I call back. "No, it's nothing."

So I am where I think I am. But . . .

I go back to the window, let the chilled air blow over me. I could pull the window shut, could close out the wind. But instead, I lean out, strain to hear the voices again. Hear them, and see the people again. . . .

"I'm not going without you, Gwen," Abe said, his face puckering. "Mama'll get mad. Please come down, before she comes out and sees you."

"And tells me I'm a disgrace, at fifteen I should know better?"

"Please, Gwenny?"

A motor sounded on the road. A car, an ancient black one, turned in, making dust cloud up from the drive. Gwen grabbed the tree limb and somersaulted down.

A boy was looking out the driver's

window. "Nice," he said to Gwen, as he stopped the car close by her. His smile was just fresh enough to bring uncertainty to Gwen's face. "Your mother home?"

Then he was getting out of the car, pulling out a black case, and setting it on the running board. "I've got some good brushes, made by the blind, good prices."

"You're a salesman?" Gwen asked. "You don't look old enough."

"Old enough for what, sugar?" he asked, his smile wider and teasing.

"I'll get my mother."

Why did he think he could talk to her that way? Maybe her mother was right, maybe she did behave in a way that asked for trouble.

"Mandeeeeeee."

Emma's calling wakes me up. I'm on my bed, and someone has closed the window and pulled one side of the quilt over me. I stay still, sorting out sounds and smells. A television commercial. Rolls and something sweet baking.

Lunch, I think, and then realize it feels too late for that. Aunt Emma must be fixing dinner. I ought to be starving, but I'm not. I'm too mixed up to want to eat.

At the window I press my face against a cold pane and try to see through my darkness into the darkness outside. I didn't imagine you, Gwen, did I? But who are you? And *when* are you?

I gather one of the curtains, feel its rough lace pattern. How can Aunt Emma say there's no one outside this window?

Monday, the day I start school, comes quickly and goes wrong before I've even left home.

I'm in the kitchen, about to ask Aunt Emma if my hair's OK, when she says, "Oh, Mandy, let me get that tag off your jeans for you." She snips threads from the corners of a sewn-on label, and I worry about what else I've missed.

My nervousness makes me extra awkward getting in the car, and my stomach hurts so bad I wonder if I'm going to be sick.

Uncle Gabriel drives and Emma sits in the front seat. "Aren't you coming, Abe?" she asks through the window.

"No, Mandy doesn't need a parade," Abe

says. He's so right. I certainly don't need a bigger production than this is going to be anyway.

I've gone to the school once already, on Friday, and met the principal and the aide who runs the resource room where I'll go in the afternoons, at least for a while. There's not a regular teacher there all the time, but just specialized ones who come in for individual kids.

When we went in on Friday, though, classes were going on and we walked through silent halls. I don't think any kids saw me.

Today, this is for real.

It's late, 12:30, but Ms. Zeisloff—she's the aide—said that maybe for the first few days coming after lunch would be best. She's waiting for us in front of the school.

She tells my aunt and uncle, "We'll take good care of Mandy."

There's a pause, and I realize Emma and Gabriel had thought they'd come in and get me settled.

"Well, I . . . Mandy?" my aunt says. Then, when I don't answer, she says, "Well, call if you need anything. We'll be back for you at three."

"You have quarters?" Gabriel asks. "For the phone?"

And suddenly it's all I can do not to say, Please don't go, don't leave me here. Their footsteps click away, down the pavement.

A door opens behind me, and Ms. Zeisloff says, "Oh, Hannah, here you are."

"Locker disaster, everything crashed out. Hi."

"Mandy," says Ms. Zeisloff, "this is Hannah Welsh."

"Hi," the girl says again, "I'm taking you around for a few days. You scared?"

I can't believe she's asked me that. What right does she have to ask how I feel? That's private and I don't even know her.

"Thank you," I say, "I will appreciate your help."

And then, like I've leaned in to invite it, this Hannah girl hugs me. Where does she get off, thinking just because I'm blind I can be hugged?

The three of us go into the school

together, Ms. Zeisloff doing a running commentary about where we are.

"This is the main hall," she says. "To get to my room we turn right and go through the outside doors at the end."

Hannah's by my side. "What's the best thing for me to do?"

"I'll take your elbow," I say, grateful she asked instead of just taking hold of my arm.

We pass a room with an open door and I hear a man talking about simultaneous equations. Some kind of blower keeps coming on and off up above us, and far away a phone is ringing.

I don't know what to do with my cane and I wish I wasn't carrying it. It screams what I am.

I try tucking it under my arm, but I realize how dumb that must look.

Sooner or later, Mandy, I tell myself, you're going to have to use this thing here. May as well be now.

I stretch the cane out in front, begin the side-to-side sweeping that's still hard for me to do, that makes my wrist and whole forearm ache. Sweep it side to side and back along the hard, smooth floor. Drag it along the wall that I'm going to have to re-member.

We reach the end of the hall.

"This door pushes out, Mandy," Ms. Zeis-loff says, and I think she's going to make me try it right then, but Hannah opens and holds it for me.

The resource room is at the other side of a courtyard, in a building by itself. "It's a temporary," Hannah says, "but it's been here as long as I can remember."

Then she's saying, "This is where I leave you, but I'll come back before school lets out."

Ms. Zeisloff and I go in together, into a room of electronic clicks and whirs, of elec-tric smells, a room just a little bit too cold.

"Everybody," Ms. Zeisloff says, rapping on something tinny-sounding for attention. Most of the clicking noises stop. I wish I knew how many people were in the room.

I wait for Ms. Zeisloff to say, "This is Mandy," but instead a boy breaks in.

"Welcome to the land of the blind, deaf, lame, maimed, outraged, and outrageous," the guy says, his voice not far from my ear. "You anything besides blind?"

33

"Ted, sit down!" Ms. Zeisloff seems exasperated but not angry.

"All right, Ms. Z., all right," says the boy. "Just welcoming the new inmate."

"Don't mind him," a girl says. "In my opinion, Ted's got some functional psychological behavioral disorder. Besides not being able to hear, of course."

It's like being in the middle of circling madness, and I want to make it hold still so I can get a clear look. I grab on to the one thing that seems a solid lie.

"If Ted's deaf, how did he hear Ms. Zeisloff?" I ask.

"Not really deaf," the girl says, "hearing impaired. Also, he reads lips. Also, he can be a real jerk."

"But, Stace," says Ted, "now we know our new inmate talks as well as walks. And she's not stupid, folks. There's a questioning brain behind those sightless eyes."

Talk about first days.

chapter 4

)))
))
))

EVERYONE'S WAITING for me
when school lets out.

I try to do the introductions right. "Hannah, this is my great-aunt Emma and my
great-uncle Gabriel and my great-uncle
Abe." I hear how awkward it sounds, those
rolling *greats*, and I wonder why I've both-
ered with them.

But if the others find them funny, they
don't say.

Aunt Emma tells Hannah she believes
she knows her mother and asks what all
Hannah does. It seems to be almost everything from student government to baby-
sitting.

I'd wondered why Hannah was messing with me, but hearing the list I can guess: I'm probably some sort of service club project.

Then we're driving home and I know Emma, Gabriel, and Abe all want me to tell them how things went. But I don't know myself and I'm too tired to sort it all out.

I sag back into the car seat.

At home I go to my room and flop on my bed. I am so tired.

For a long time the afternoon happens again and again in my mind, names and voices and snatches of talk and how the bumps of one, two, and three felt under my fingers.

"Some people think braille is on its way out," Ms. Zeisloff told me, "but I don't believe that."

Teaching me braille will be the job of one of the itinerant teachers, a woman who'll work with me for a couple of hours three afternoons a week beginning Wednesday or Thursday.

Meanwhile, Ms. Z. says she knows just enough to get me started.

Braille dots under my fingertips . . .

I think of Gwen, whoever she is. Gwen, whose fingertips dragged in summer dirt when she hung upside down from a tree limb.

Had I made her up?

I go to my window, open it. Run my hand down a lace curtain.

It's just a curtain, I'm thinking, when the breeze quickens, pulls it from my hand, pulls on me.

This time I lean into the dark wind, give myself over to it. In another moment I'm back all those years again, back to seeing, watching another girl in another time. . . .

Gwen snatched up her shoes and ran around to the back of the house, before her mother could come to the door and see her. She slipped into the kitchen, turned the radio on softly, and then went back outside.

Sitting against the house in the cool shade, her bare legs on the cold, rough concrete of the side walkway, she waited for her program to come on. The salesman was here with a lot of things for her mother to look at. Maybe Gwen would have a whole half hour, long enough to hear an entire program, which didn't happen often.

But news came on instead, more about Korea.

Gwen had heard it first the evening before, from Abe, who'd heard it on the radio and run to tell. "We're at war," he had shouted. "The radio says we're at war and we got eight of their planes, but they didn't shoot down any of ours."

"Nonsense," their mother had said. "Don't make things up."

But of course the story had been in this morning's paper, and then all their mother could say was, "Well, here we go again."

Gwen thought about the salesman. Would he have to go to war? How old was he, eighteen maybe? Old enough to be drafted?

A screen door slapped shut in the front. He was leaving.

Gwen ran along the side of the house.

"Bye," she called, stopping him as he got in his car. "I just . . ." She searched for something to say. Stepped closer. "My mother buy any brushes?"

"You got a name, sugar?" he asked.

She looked carefully, decided his smile was not a smirk.

"Gwen," she said. "What's yours?"

"Paul."

Paul started his car, getting the motor to catch on the third try. Wiggled the stick shift into reverse. "Be seeing you, Gwendolyn," he said. "Don't do anything I wouldn't do."

"Gwen, not Gwendolyn. And I don't see how you'll be seeing me."

"Thursday," he said. "Thursday I sell soap. I'll be back."

"Mandy," Aunt Emma says, giving my shoulder a light shake. "You've got to get up now if you're not going to be late."

I wish I didn't have to go.

It's Thursday morning, my fourth day of school, but so far I've only gone for afternoons, only dealt with the resource room. Kids are in there on varying, overlapping schedules, but I'm starting to get them figured out.

I've gotten to know Ted, who really is more funny than mean, as long as you understand his sense of humor. I've also met Marissa, who's the only other one in the resource room with what she calls a "vision impairment." Marissa can see a lot, only very fuzzy, and she doesn't want to have anything to do with me.

I'm not sure why Stace and the other boy are there. Ms. Z. doesn't give a lot of time for talking.

But anyway, today . . . Today I start my regular schedule.

First period I've got math, the same class as Hannah. We go in together, early, and she introduces me to Mr. Casie, the teacher.

I ask where my desk is, but Mr. Casie's got a table all set up for me instead. There's a computer on it, which he says he's ordered earphones and some software for.

"There's also an electrical outlet for whatever else you need, Mandy," he says. "I suppose you'll be bringing a tape recorder?"

I have a sudden vision of Mandy the camel, hunching along the hall under a load of equipment.

"I don't know," I say. "Maybe."

I wish he'd let me slip into a normal desk

like everyone else, but before I can ask there's a bell ringing and the room is filled with the racket of talking kids.

Hannah squeezes my arm. "You'll do OK," she says.

I find the chair and sit, wonder where to look. Wish maybe I had a tape recorder after all because it would be something I could be busy with. I wonder if everyone's staring at me?

I hold my hands tight together; I will not put them up to check my hair, check if my collar is flat.

It seems forever before the bell rings again and the room gets quiet.

Then Mr. Casie is telling the class who I am, and I say "Hi," hoping I'm talking in the right direction.

"Man," says some boy, "math's hard enough when you can see the stuff."

But Mr. Casie's telling everyone what page to turn to and at the same time telling me to try to follow along.

Then I realize the class is doing statistics, new material for them but stuff I've had before.

I think, Mandy, you know this.

One thing I learned years ago—the more scared I am, the better it is to jump in fast. I wait for a question that I'm sure about the answer to and put up my hand.

"Mandy?" Mr. Casie calls on me.

"You don't try to control variables in a random sampling," I say. "That's the whole point of random samples—the randomness evens out the variables."

The boy who said "Man" before says "Man" again, this time like he's impressed.

My heart's pounding and I hold my hands in my lap, hope nobody can see how they're shaking.

"Very good, Mandy," says Mr. Casie, as if I haven't done anything special.

chapter 5

HANNAH TUGS ME through the halls the way some mothers tug their children, like attachments that are a normal part of things. I hold her arm, but she does the tugging.

I've wondered how I'll find a bathroom, but we go to one between classes, without me asking. Hannah warns me, "The seat's wet, don't sit down." Then she says, "Sorry. Tell me when I overdo."

How am I supposed to figure out how to deal with Hannah when she answers what's on my mind before I say it?

The rest of the morning goes by in a growing blur of noise and smells and bits of

43

touch too small for me to know what I'm feeling.

Changing classes is the worst, and the crowds in the halls make it impossible for me to use my cane. We get to both English and geography late; the English teacher passes over it, but I hear the geography teacher give an exaggerated sigh.

He spends the period drilling the class on a current events map, making them find places mentioned in news stories: Seattle and Cincinnati, Yellowstone Park and the Columbia River Basin. And after class, when Hannah and I are leaving, he says, "Mandy, perhaps this class is not the best placement for you. This class is based on knowing maps."

"I can do geography without seeing your maps," I tell him. "I've lived in half the places you talked about."

Jerk, I think. I'll decide for myself what I can and cannot do.

But fourth period I sit out a gym class because the teacher says she's not allowed to have me participate in any activities until the modified program she's worked out gets official approval.

After that it's lunch. Somehow Hannah guesses how much I need quiet.

"Instead of the cafeteria," she says, "maybe we could eat in Ms. Zeisloff's room. You can have part of my sandwich, if you didn't bring anything."

The resource room is locked, but the day is warm enough for us to eat outside. We sit on the grass, our backs against the building. It's blessedly silent.

Slowly the welter of stuff that is muddling my mind drains away, until for the first time in hours I feel in control. I let my thoughts drift away from school, drift to Gwen and to what I've learned about her.

The Korean War started at the end of June in 1950. Ted looked it up for me in the encyclopedia. So now I know the time that I go to when I lean past the curtains. I know when Gwen lived, this girl who pulls me through time to the year she was my age.

And I've done my math. Uncle Abe would have been about five then, which fits since he must be about fifty now, or maybe a little older.

For I'm sure that is who that boy is, Gwen's little brother. He has Uncle Abe's way of talking, words going just a bit uphill and down. The house that the two of them live in is the house that I'm living in now. And the tree where I first saw Gwen hanging by her knees still stands, only it's much, much bigger now. So big I can't put my arms halfway around it, and the ground under it is gnarled with pushed-up roots.

What I don't know is who Gwen is. I mean, I realize she must be a great-aunt of mine, a sister of my great-uncles Abe and Gabriel, and of my grandmother, whose name was Margaret. I just don't know where Gwen *fits*.

I haven't heard Emma or the uncles mention her. No one has said, "Is Gwen coming for Christmas?" or "Is Gwen's gift in the mail yet?" And you'd think they would. I've always imagined that's what real families do.

Maybe she's dead like my grandmother?

Sooner or later, I'll ask.

But not yet. For now, I like the mystery of her, like the mystery of seeing her in another time. For now, I like having one thing that is all mine, privately mine, that no one else knows about.

"Mandy." Hannah's voice breaks into my thoughts. "Are you sleeping or daydreaming? You look like you're miles away."

"Sorry," I say. I keep my voice light. "I guess I did drift pretty far off."

When I get home Thursday I go to my room, eager to leave my own world and be lost again in Gwen's. I lean out my window into the breeze, lean out and wait to hear the calling.

The breeze doesn't change, and I stay with just myself, alone.

Instead of seeing Gwen, I think of my mom and me, years ago. I remember how one morning she sent me off to one of the jillion different grade schools I went to.

"Knock 'em dead, kid," she said, even though I'd been at that particular school long enough for us both to know I wasn't going to.

She pinned a plastic Christmas tree pin on my coat. It was just the kind that kids would laugh at, but I waited until I was down the street to put it in my pocket.

I remember the hurt of that morning.

A girl named Aimee and I were picked to

stay in during recess and make paper chains to decorate the room. Aimee cut red and green strips while I pasted circle through circle, as fast as I could. Soon the smell of wet paste was all around and a chain of colored paper bunched and rustled on the floor.

We started giggling, and then Aimee draped a piece of chain across the bust of a Roman emperor. I roped more of it around my waist, and Aimee tore off enough to make a necklace for herself. We were having fun, and I was sure she liked me.

Then a couple of boys looked in the window at us. Aimee must not have wanted them thinking we were friends, because she took the chain from around her neck and went back to cutting paper strips, and she didn't say another word.

Saturday comes. Hannah telephones even before I'm out of bed. She wants to know if I want to go to a football game. "It's a play-off," she says. "The whole school will be there."

"So what do I do at a football game?" I ask.

"Walk around. Talk. See people."

"Like I could."

Hannah says, "Knock it off, Mandy. That's sick."

I'm learning Hannah does not put up with my sounding sorry for myself.

"I'll think about it."

"Mandy, the game starts at one."

"OK, OK. I'll go."

"I'll pick you up," she says. "I got my license last month."

"That's when you turned sixteen?" I ask.

"Yeah."

I hang up before I realize I probably should have thanked her.

I go back to my room and make my bed.

Go to my dressing table and touch my mom's picture. "Do you know what I'm doing, Mom? Going to a football game. Isn't that a laugh?"

But I don't hear Mom laughing back, and I realize I can't quite remember what her laugh sounded like. Tears in my eyes, I put down her picture, go to close my window.

Without warning, I find myself being pulled to Gwen, being pulled again into the wind behind the curtains, into Gwen's life that summer of 1950. . . .

"*Pill bug, pill bug, curl up tight.*"

"It's '*Ladybug. Fly home.*'"

"But these are pill bugs, Gwen. Want to see my pill bug circus?"

Abe was stretched out on his stomach, planting toothpicks tipped with tiny bright flags in a circle in the dusty earth. A gray pill bug crawled tanklike to one of them, then felt its way around.

"How come he doesn't curl up at the toothpick, like he does when he touches my finger, Gwen?"

"Ask Dad."

Just then the screen door opened and their father stepped onto the porch, walked down the steps to the car. Abe called, "Dad, come see. I'm training pill bugs."

"Not now. Maybe later."

Abe arranged pebbles inside the circle of flags. "Seats, Gwen, for the audience. How long do you think Dad will be?"

"That depends on where he's gone."

"Do you think he's driving all the way to town?"

A few minutes later, Abe said, "I'm going to let my pill bugs go. I think they're tired."

Gwen watched him run off, then straightened two of the toothpick flagpoles. This was the most restless, boring summer. And hot. It felt like something should happen.

She wished something would happen.

Except she knew nothing would, it never did. That salesman, Paul, hadn't even come back, when he'd almost promised.

What would it be like, Gwen wondered, to be Abe? To be little again?

No, maybe that wasn't the question. Abe always had something to do. Was that because he was little and there was still stuff left that he thought was exciting? Or because he was a boy, and there really was?

"Gwen, come in here." Her mother spoke from the window above. "The beans need snapping now or I won't have them ready in time to eat. And wash off your knees. When are you going to start acting your age?"

"Never."

"What did you say?"

"I said I'm coming."

I should tell her, thought Gwen, that I don't see any point in growing up, just to spend Saturday afternoon cooking so I can serve supper exactly at 6:00 P.M. Saturday evening. I should tell her I'm never, ever going to think it's something to be proud of, just to get a meal ready on time.

"I'm coming," Gwen yelled again, louder than necessary.

She and her mother worked without talking, except once her mother said, "Gwen, did your father say where he was going?" and a little later, "I wonder what's keeping your father."

He still wasn't back at 5:30 or 5:40, nor at 5:50, when her mother called to everyone to wash their hands and come to the table.

They sat—her mother at her end, Gwen on one side, Abe and the older boy on the other—and waited.

Six o'clock came, and the chair at the far end, the only chair with arms, was still empty.

"Well," said Gwen's mother. "Well." She asked Gwen to say grace.

———

"What happened? What happened to your father?" I call.

One instant I'm with Gwen and the next I am alone in my room, and it has happened so fast I feel light-headed.

I have to know, Did Gwen lose her dad, the way I lost Mom? Did he get killed in some accident and never tell Abe why pill bugs curl up?

I wait until my head clears. Then I stretch as far out into the wind as I can.

"Gwen," I call. "Gwen? Please answer. Tell me what happened."

I think of another question. "And where was my grandmother? Why wasn't there another girl at the table?"

I'm grabbed from behind and jerked inside.

"Mandy! Mandy, don't you know how far down the ground is?"

It's Uncle Gabriel, and his voice is loud and angry and shaky, all at once. "Mandy, this room is three stories up. Don't ever lean out the window like that."

He's still holding my arm, even though I'm standing up straight now. I shake myself free. Turn deliberately until the back of my waist is pressed flat against the sill and my shoulders arch into emptiness.

"Don't worry about me," I say. "I won't fall."

"Mandy, you get away from that window. You're as stubborn as . . . Mandy, we're going to take care of you whether you like it or not."

"As stubborn as who?"

"Whether you like it or not."

"Who?"

But Gabriel pulls me in, shuts the window hard.

"Emma's made an early lunch for you, Mandy," he says. "Better fix your hair before you go down. She'll think you've been in a wind."

chapter 6

)))
))
))

WHEN HANNAH COMES for me I
try to just leave, but no way. Aunt Emma is
so excited about me going to the football
game that Hannah must realize this is the
first time I've gone out, except shopping and
to school.

And Uncle Gabriel wants us to sit down
while he reads a newspaper story about the
two teams. "You should know who the play-
ers are," he says.

"Hannah probably already knows," I tell
him.

"That's OK," Hannah says. "Does it say
our school's expected to win?"

When we're out in the car, I tell her she

didn't have to do that, pretend she was interested.

"I *was* interested. And besides, it's touching how much they care about what you're doing. You're lucky, Mandy."

Me, lucky? How can she say something so dumb? "Want to trade places?" I ask.

I expect to her to say, "Shut up. That's sick." Instead she says, "Maybe. Families, anyway."

Then she lightens up. "Want to meet mine? Mom said I could ask you over for dinner and to spend the night."

I don't know until we get to the game that we're meeting anyone else. The football field is behind the high school, on the far side of the parking lot. As we walk over from the car, Hannah's saying, "Mandy, this is Charla," and, "Mandy, Rosa," and, "Blakney, Mandy."

I try to hear how their individual voices sound, but they don't say enough words for me to get down which is which. Within minutes the talk is a jumble and the only person I can pick out is Hannah.

I'm moving along OK, using my cane, one hand barely touching Hannah's arm. Then one of the other girls says, "They're lining up for kickoff. Let's hurry."

I walk faster, stumble. Someone says, "Hannah, why don't we meet you in the stands?"

I can feel my face flaming red. I want to tell Hannah she doesn't have to wait for me, but I can't. Where would I go if she left me?

Someone else has stayed back, too, and I hear Hannah call her Charla.

This girl, Charla, she wants to talk about a dance that's coming up, a girl-ask-guy holiday thing. "You're taking Ryan, Hannah?" she asks.

"I guess."

Then Charla says, "Mandy, are you going to ask someone?"

Is she joking? I replay her words, listen for the emphasis on *you* that would give her away. It's not there. What's wrong with her?

"No," I say. "No one to ask."

"How about Ted?" she asks. "Don't you two hang around some?"

Now I get it. I open my mouth to say,

"Pair up the misfits?" but before I get a word out, Hannah pinches me.

"Shut up," she whispers. "Just don't say it."

After the game, which is more loud than anything and I'm glad when it's over, Hannah and I go to my house for my stuff. Aunt Emma acts like I'm going on a world cruise, instead of just to spend the night, and I'm embarrassed that she lets Hannah know she thinks this is such a big thing.

Hannah lives in town. We have to go back almost to the school to get to her place.

"Tell me what your house is like," I ask when we drive up.

"It's brick, one floor. Looks like all the other houses around here."

I stand inside the front door for a moment and listen to how far Hannah shouts when she calls, "We're here." Listen for echoes. Notice cold coming up from the tile under my feet. Do not smell dust or mold. It's a clean-feeling, hollow-seeming house.

"Hello, Mandy."

Hannah's mother has a voice that is perfect and polite and without one bit of niceness. The voice of the kind of woman who will pry right into me.

"Now," she says, "you're Emma's niece? I don't remember ever meeting your mother." She makes it a question that has to be answered.

I wish I could wrap my arms around my insides, keep her eyes off my mom and me and my privacy.

"Emma is my great-aunt," I say. "But it sounds silly to call her Great-aunt Emma, so I say Aunt Emma . . ." I hear myself babbling, but I can't stop. "You've never met my mother. We never got down here."

Dinner is awful.

It's in a dining room, with a cloth on the table, and Hannah's parents are both there and her little brother. And nobody says a word about how nice the table looks, so I know this isn't just for company.

The food's spaghetti, which is hard for me to manage because of the sauce, and I eat very slowly and carefully, cutting small sections. Once Hannah reaches over and does something to my plate, and another time her mother whispers, "Hannah," and Hannah whispers, "Mandy, use your napkin."

Her father wants to know about the equipment I've got, and I get talking about how the school computer has an add-on that synthesizes speech, how whatever is on the screen is read out loud. It really is a neat machine, and he seems interested.

But then Hannah's little brother says, "Those computer voices are so bad," and he's right, of course.

After dinner Hannah and I go to her room, where she turns on some music, tosses a cushion at me, and says, "So, want to hear about Ted?"

"Ted?"

"Or anybody else. I thought maybe you've been around long enough you must be getting people sorted out. That maybe you'd have questions about them?"

"Or about you?" I say, I guess a little mean. But I am curious about this Hannah who lives in a perfectly clean house. Hannah, who is all the things I've never been, even nice. "That Ryan that Charla talked about, he's your boyfriend?"

"Yeah, sort of. No. I don't know."

"He's the guy who scored all those points today?"

"Yeah."

"Figures," I say, but she goes on like she doesn't hear me.

"We're friends. It just makes it easier if we say we're a couple. Takes the pressure off, from everybody else, I mean."

I think about that. Nod like I know what she means, even though I'm not sure.

"Did you have a boyfriend," she asks, "before you came here?"

"You mean when I could see?" But Hannah lets that pass, too, and I've got to think of a better answer.

"There wasn't really time," I say. "Mom and I moved around a lot."

"Maybe you'll find one here," she says.

"Ted?"

"He's good-looking." She puts a bowl in my lap. "Popcorn, made it last night."

"Would you go out with Ted?" I ask.

"No. But not why you're thinking. He's so smart he scares me. And it's hard to tell when he's joking."

Yeah.

We talk for a while, then Hannah has me

move over so she can reach under her bed. "Ever play with a Ouija board?" she asks. "We can get us both boyfriends."

I hear her click off the light. "It works better in the dark. There's enough moonlight to read the letters."

Then Hannah shows me how to rest my fingers on the plastic disk. She says in this phony fortune-teller voice, "Oh tell us, Great Ouija, who will Mandy's love be?"

Nothing happens. Hannah whispers, "Just wait."

I wait, feeling foolish at first, and then holding in giggles and trying to make myself believe.

The marker wiggles right, joggles left, suddenly moves fast three or four inches.

"It's stopped on X," says Hannah. "Mandy, concentrate."

Her mother opens the door. "Hannah," she begins, "why don't you find something Mandy can . . . ," but switches to, "Don't stay up late, girls."

"We won't," Hannah says. We wait for the door to close before we go back to the Ouija.

The board tells us Hannah is going to

62

marry someone with the initials B. T. S., and we can't think of anybody at school with those initials unless it's Boone Simon. Hannah says nobody would ever marry Boone Simon, who never takes a shower, and maybe the Ouija board is nonsense.

A while later we're lying a few feet apart in twin beds. I'm wondering if Hannah is asleep when she says, "Mandy, wouldn't it be great if you really could ask about the future and get answers?"

"Maybe," I say.

"My dad says his dad saw a ghost once, who warned him not to go fishing and he did anyway and almost drowned."

When I don't say anything, she asks, "You ever know anybody who saw a ghost?"

"No," I say. And then, I don't know why, maybe because I've never before in my life stayed overnight with a friend, talked in the dark like this, I say, "but there's this girl, Gwen . . ."

I tell about the lace curtains, about the voices, about Gwen and Abe and Paul, and Hannah doesn't think I'm crazy. She says what happens—how I lean out the window and become Gwen, become her and watch her at the same time—is one of the most exciting things she has ever heard.

"Sometimes when I'm doing something I get the feeling I'm watching me do it," she says. "Is that how Gwen is?"

"Sort of," I say, looking for a better way to tell her. "More like when you read a book, and you're seeing what the main character is doing, but you're inside and thinking her thoughts at the same time."

"Do you think Paul's going to come back? Or Gwen's dad?"

"I don't know."

Then Hannah says, "You must miss being able to read, if you used to do it a lot."

"There are substitutes," I say. "Books on tape. Braille, if I ever learn it. But, of course, it's not the same thing."

And a long time later, Hannah says, "I wish something like Gwen would happen to me, but I guess it won't. I'm too ordinary."

And the way she says it, I realize she means I must be somebody special. That she wishes, at least for this, that she could be me.

And, lying in shared darkness, I take that

thought and turn it over, and don't try to throw it away.

Sometime later, I don't know how late, we fall asleep. I wake up once, listen to Hannah's slow, quiet-whistle breathing. What a nice, nice night.

In the morning Hannah and I sit around the family room in bathrobes, drinking hot chocolate while her father reads the funnies. Every few minutes he laughs and says, "Girls, listen to this."

Hannah's brother must be sitting next to him. "Dad," he says a couple of times, "you're leaving things out."

I think we're all sorry when Hannah's mom comes to tell us we can't wait any longer to dress. "Mandy," she adds, "we'll drive you home before we go to church, so no one has to come for you."

"Thank you," I say, "if it's not any trouble."

"Certainly, it's trouble, but I wouldn't have offered if I weren't willing to take the trouble." The way she says it makes me flush and wonder how I was rude.

When they let me off, Hannah asks me, "Can I come over later?" but her mother says, "Not today. I need you at home today, Hannah."

It's not until a couple of hours have gone by that I realize I wasn't rude asking how much trouble it would be to take me home. It was Hannah's mother who was rude, with her answer.

I try to do homework in the afternoon, but I can't concentrate. I end up standing at my dressing table. I find the photo of my mother, move my hand to the smaller frame next to it, the one of my grandfather in his airman's jacket. I run my finger down until I'm touching right where his face, blurred and almost lost in shadow, would be. "That's you that didn't come home to dinner?"

Except as soon as I say it, I know I'm wrong. The photo is of my grandfather. The man whose dining room chair stayed empty, Gwen and Abe's dad, and Gabriel's, he would be my great-grandfather.

It's hard to keep straight.

And where was Margaret, my grandmother? Why hadn't she been at the dinner table with the others? Had she already left home? Gone off to have the baby she would put up for adoption? The baby who would be my mom.

"Mandy," Aunt Emma calls, "would you like some hot chocolate with us?"

"Yes, please," I call.

I think again of asking the uncles about Gwen. If I ask, will I risk losing her? Might that somehow stop me from going back to her time?

Be honest, Mandy girl, I think. Aren't you scared of what you might say if your uncles want to know why you're asking about Gwen? Scared you might blurt out, "Well, every so often I lean past the lace curtains and skip off to 1950?"

Right, go from being Mandy who's just blind to being Mandy who's got multiple problems. There'll be a million more conferences with doctors and counselors, and then the next time there's a student admitted to Ms. Z.'s room, Ted can do a new introduction:

"And this is Mandy," he'll say, "blind, PLUS she entertains the notion she can time-travel. Tell our new inmate, Mandy, is hindsight better than no sight?"

"Oh, shut up, Ted, and sit . . ."

"MANDEEE!" Aunt Emma calls.

Maybe I really am losing it. "Coming. Right now."

No, I won't ask who Gwen is.

chapter 7

♪ ♪ ♪
♪ ♪ ♪
♪ ♪

WHEN I GO to Gwen again I go to another Texas morning. This time the passage is slower, as if the wind can hardly stir. It is a passage to a morning later in that summer. . . .

Gwen asked, "Do you want the pillow-cases sprinkled, Mama?"

"Certainly."

Her mother was ironing, going piece by piece through a basket of rolled, damp linens. Linens they could no longer afford to send out.

It was early, but already the day was

heating up. They were working on the screened-in side porch.

"Nobody sees pillowcases," Gwen said.

"Nobody sees your shirttails, either, but you keep them ironed."

Gwen traced a monogram with one finger. Her mother's maiden name initials. Probably embroidered before she got married, maybe even before she got engaged.

"Mama, do you miss Daddy?"

"What kind of question is that?"

"But do you?"

"Gone is gone, and there's no use crying over spilt milk."

"But, Mama . . . I was wondering . . . how are we going to live? I mean . . . do we have any . . . ?"

Gwen watched her mother's lips tighten into a straight line. "I will be starting work next week, Gwen. The bank has hired me to be a receptionist."

Gwen rolled the last two pillowcases together and tucked them into the bottom of the basket. "Do you want to do that?"

"*Want* doesn't come into it."

"But, Mama . . . how do you feel about it?" The words rushed out. "About Daddy leaving us, and you having to go out and work, and us . . . What are you going to do about us? Abe and . . ."

"*Feel?*" Her mother repeated the word as though she was trying out a strange sound. "*Feel* doesn't come into it, either. And you can help with the boys in the afternoons, you're big enough."

Gwen thought about Abe, who had hardly talked at all since he'd realized that their father wouldn't be coming back. She'd found what was left of his pill bug circus scattered behind an oleander bush, every toothpick broken and every tiny flag wadded up.

Gabriel seemed less affected, bicycling off most days to see his friends. Still, Gwen had occasionally caught him looking puzzled in a way that didn't seem right for a kid.

But now her mother was setting down the iron. "Oh, that dust!" she exclaimed as a car turned in the drive. "Gwen, is that that salesman again? Didn't Gabriel say he was here yesterday?"

Paul called, "Good morning," as he got out of the car. Then he opened the screen door without being asked and came onto the porch.

Gwen's mother picked up her iron. "What are you selling this time?"

"Nothing. I came to see if I could take Gwen for an ice cream."

Gwen's mother looked surprised, and then like she'd tasted something bad. "How do you know Gwen? Gwen is too young to go on a date."

"It's not a date, Mama," Gwen said. "It's for ice cream."

She ran down to the car, heard Paul following, even while he was calling back things that sounded polite.

Gwen whispered, "Let's go, before she says no."

They were out the driveway, out of sight of the porch, before Paul looked sideways, met her with a smile.

"You really want ice cream?"

I wake up cold on Monday morning, cold air blowing in on me from the window. Aunt Emma has stopped asking me why I leave it wide open at night.

"Fresh air never hurt anyone," Gabriel

told her the last time she asked. "When I was in the army, we always kept windows open in the billets."

Abe said I was cleaning spiderwebs. I finally figured out he meant I was clearing cobwebs from my brain.

I wiggle further into the covers, my thoughts shifting from the kids at school to Gwen and Paul, drifting from football games to a band of woods beside a summer lake. Cobwebby woods. Nice woods, I think, although . . .

"Hey, lazy bones, don't you know what time it is?"

It's Uncle Gabriel, at my door. He's gotten me this talking clock that you hit and it tells you the time.

I grab for it, hear a perfectly flat, absolutely one-tone voice say, "Seven-oh-clock— oh-seven-hundred-and-fifteen-seconds."

At school Hannah is full of plans for finding out about Gwen. "Maybe I can come over to your house and go through photo albums with you," she says. "Maybe we'll find Gwen's name written on a picture."

"I've about decided to ask Aunt Emma

who was in my uncles' family. See if she mentions Gwen."

"And if she doesn't?"

"I don't know. Go to Plan Two, I guess."

"Which is?"

"Hannah, I don't know. I don't have a Plan Two. Probably Aunt Emma will tell me Gwen's a retired librarian in San Antonio or Dallas and that will be that."

But now Hannah's the one who wants to be all mysterious and makes me promise we'll try to find out ourselves about Gwen before I ask. I get the idea that what she really wants is an excuse to go home with me instead of to her own home. And, of course, I should have her over since I spent the night at her house.

"OK," I say, "it's OK with me."

Hannah leaves me at the door to my gym class. "I'll be at your place about four," she says. "And Mandy . . . let's not tell anybody else about Gwen. She can be our secret?"

I try to remember if I've ever had a secret with another girl before. I don't think so.

Not that I'm sharing this one quite all the way. I don't think I want to tell Hannah about that last time, how Gwen and Paul were kissing in the car. It seems sort of . . . personal.

The tardy bell startles me and I turn quickly, groping for a handle on a closed door that won't push in. I find a knob instead, pull the door open, and a second later bang my stomach against something solid.

I cautiously run my hand along it until I realize it's a sink. My shoulder hits something that clatters to the floor.

This isn't the gym.

I try to think what I know about the wall by the gym door. What's along it? Hannah hasn't said there's a girls' room. What if I've barged into a boys' bathroom? I take a panicky step and knock something else over.

Then my hand finds the stiff bristles of a brush and next to that a wet cloth. I'm in a cleaning closet.

Relief runs through me and then my cheeks go flaming hot. I back out, wondering who's seen Mandy's latest mistake.

But the hall's quiet. Maybe nobody has.

I say a little thank-you as I search for another door. I find one and open it, and this time I listen for gymnasium echoes before I go any farther.

After lunch Ted's waiting for me outside Ms. Zeisloff's room. I think we must look like a couple, standing there.

"You want people to see us together?" I ask. "The deaf boy reading the lips of the blind girl listening . . ."

"I just wanted you to know I'm not coming to class today. I'm in the middle of a project that I've got to finish before it sets, and I've got a pass to work in the art room."

"So why are you telling me?"

And as fast as I say it, I feel guilty in case I've hurt Ted's feelings, which is stupid, but I about fall over myself trying to make things right. "Ms. Z.'s will be boring without you. I didn't know you did art."

"Yeah, well . . ." His voice trails off.

"Mandy and Ted," Ms. Z. says, "time to get started."

Ted must show her his pass. She says, "All right," and I hear her go inside.

The path is quiet now because the period's begun. I suddenly realize this is about as good a time as I'm going to get to ask Ted to the holiday dance. I wish my hands weren't so clammy. I hope my face isn't getting blotchy red, the way it does some-times when I'm nervous.

"Ted, the dance that's coming up . . . Would you like to go?" I say, the words spill-ing out.

I should have said it differently. What if he doesn't understand that I'm inviting him?

I add, "With me, I mean?"

"So everyone can watch the blind girl be-ing led around by the deaf boy who can't hear the music?" But he's laughing as he says it, a friendly laugh.

"Something like that," I answer.

For the briefest moment, Ted takes my hand, and I don't know if he's holding it or shaking it. Actually, the way he does it, so fumbling and awkward, I doubt if he knows.

Ted says, "I accept with pleasure."

I go inside and my itinerant teacher, Ms. Thorn, wants to work with me on a new set of braille exercises that Ms. Z. is generating.

"Things going OK, Mandy?" Ms. Thorn asks while we wait for the embosser to fin-ish the page of bumps and spaces. "Did you get the math tapes we ordered?"

She goes over what I'm doing, class by class, before she says, "All right. Now, let's see how you and your braillewriter are getting along."

The brailler reminds me of an old typewriter, the kind people had before electric ones and before computers. There's just one row of keys, three on the left and three on the right, that you press to form the six dots of a braille cell. In the middle is a space bar that you work with your thumbs.

I feed in a sheet of paper and get started on today's exercise, which is a page full of words like *cap, cat, can, pan.* I'm to read them off the sheet from the embosser and then duplicate them on the braillewriter.

Grade-one braille, Ms. Thorn calls what I'm doing, working letter by letter rather than with the code for common words and letter combinations; that is grade two.

It may be called grade one, but what I'm struggling with is worse than it was learning to read print when I was six years old and really in the first grade.

"I don't know why I have to learn this stuff, anyway," I say. "I can type my work on a computer like everyone else and then just listen to it."

Ms. Thorn adjusts the way my left hand

is positioned on the brailler keys. "But Mandy," she says, "how are you going to check your writing with a speech synthesizer? Or revise it? Do it letter by letter? Word by word? You won't be able to see punctuation or word spacing."

"I can't see this, either."

"You will, Mandy," Ms. Thorn says. "One day you'll be able to see braille the way I see print on a page. That's what braille does, Mandy. It lets you *see*."

Promises and hype, I think. I wonder how much is just sales pitch.

But Ms. Thorn doesn't sound like a salesperson, and I want to believe.

"OK," I tell her. "But I may be ancient before I get it learned."

Ms. Thorn coaches me for a while as I make *cat* and *can* with the braillewriter. Then she tells me she's going to check on Marissa and I should call if I need help.

Pan. My fingers hover over the keys as I try to picture the dot pattern that makes the letter *p*. A is easy: one dot, top left in the braille cell. Four dots for *n*. I pull the lever to ratchet my paper up one line and go back to the exercise page.

What I find seems too wide a pattern for the domino-like braille cell. I start to call, "Ms. Thorn, there's a mistake." But then I remember about the number sign, how a backward *L* of dots changes what follows from a letter to a number. I find the backward *L* and then the single dot that it turns from *a* into *1*.

I'm pleased I figured it out, but I don't think my teachers should be throwing me trick problems that I might take for mistakes.

I hunch over the brailler and think about Ted and me. About Gwen and Paul. About that ice-cream trip that was really a drive into woods by a lake.

What have I gotten myself into?

I asked Ted. Actually asked him. And he said he'd go.

My stomach knots up. How am I going to keep from making a fool of myself? I won't fit in, not at a dance.

Except . . . I like the way he took my hand.

I hear Ms. Thorn behind me, but I pretend to be so busy that I don't realize she's there. I hope it doesn't show, how mixed up I feel inside.

chapter 8

‏♩ ♩
♩ ♩
♩ ♩

AT HOME Uncle Gabriel puts some money into my hand. Fifty dollars, he tells me, all in tens. "I figured you'd want to start Christmas shopping early the way Emma always does," he says.

I must look absolutely out of it, because he adds, "Don't forget something for your aunt. Emma's been carrying on about Christmas this year like I've never seen her before."

"She needn't carry on for me."

But Gabriel continues as if I haven't said a word. "You know, we almost had a baby once, your aunt Emma and me, a little girl that died at birth. Your being here—for your aunt it's kind of like being given the daughter she was never able to have."

I know Gabriel means well, wants to let me know I'm not just a burden. But instead he's making me miss my mother so much. Christmastime . . . of all the times, that was when we were the most separate from everyone else, and it made us close. It was like we held each other up in a lonely wind.

Gabriel's still talking about Christmas presents when Hannah shows up. He says, "Maybe you girls can go shopping together."

Hannah says, "Sure. It'll be fun."

When we're alone, though, I say, "I don't need your help, Hannah. I can pick things out without help."

"Mandy," she says, "I know you can, but how are you going to get to the stores? Walk ten miles? Are you ready to find your way around by yourself?"

That last is not a fair question because she knows I'm not.

"Besides," she says, "shopping alone is no fun. Now where are the photo albums?"

I hear her go into the living room, and her voice comes back from several feet away.

"Mandy," she says, "why don't you give yourself a Christmas present and stop being so prickly?"

"I'm not prickly."

"You are."

We find albums on the bottom shelf of the television cabinet. Hannah pages through the one she says looks the oldest, searching for photos with names under them. Mostly, she says, the pictures aren't labeled, or the labels say things like "My recital dress."

Aunt Emma comes into the room, bringing us hot chocolate. "I won't bother you girls." Then, "Oh, look at that. Mandy, Hannah's found a picture of your uncles at the beach at Galveston. Abe's so little he's in a diaper instead of a swimsuit."

A moment more and she's down on the floor with us, which I know because I hear the bones in her knees crack as she lowers herself. "My," she says, "I haven't looked at these pictures in years."

"Here's another one," says Hannah. "They're with a girl."

"That's Gwen. Their big sister Gwen."

My heart feels as if it's going to explode out of my chest. I want to ask . . . except my cheeks are suddenly so stiff, I don't think I can talk.

But Hannah says, as cool as anything, "She's pretty, like Mandy."

"She was Mandy's grandmother," Emma says. "Mandy takes after her."

"But . . ." Hannah's voice trails off.

I know I should say something, should correct Emma. Should say, "Gwen wasn't my grandmother, my grandmother's name was Margaret." But I can't, not with Hannah there. How can I let Hannah know, Hannah with her mother and father and brother and dining room tablecloth, that my family is so spaced we can't even agree on my grandmother's name?

So I don't say anything, only huddle quietly while Hannah and Emma talk on and on.

Later, in my room, Hannah says, "Mandy, do you think maybe you've just *imagined* seeing Gwen? That you've known about your grandmother all along, stories tucked in your subconscious? That being here has made them come out?"

"I haven't been lying," I say, and I feel my face get hot. "I never heard any stories about my grandmother at all because my mom didn't know any to tell."

Hannah waits, her unasked questions filling my bedroom.

"Look," I blurt out, "my mother was put up for adoption when she was a baby. She didn't know anything about her real family, not until a couple of weeks before she died."

I hear Hannah walk over to my window and open it. I imagine her leaning out while she tries to decide what to believe. Her voice comes back, muffled. "Yeah," she says, "families can sure get messed up."

And an instant later she's plopping down on my bed, starting to talk about the dance. "Do you and Ted want to double with Ryan and me? I'll drive, since it's girl-ask-guy."

We don't say another word about families, not mine, not hers. It's like we've agreed to let it rest for now.

We go through my closet, and Hannah says maybe I'd better see if I can get something new because the holiday dance is pretty dressy. "Or you can borrow something of mine," she says. "We're about the same size."

Our talk is surface talk, but even that's a struggle to keep up with. Most of my mind is turned inward, trying to understand how Gwen could be my grandmother.

After Hannah leaves I go to the kitchen, where Aunt Emma is peeling carrots. She shaves off curls for me to nibble.

"You said Gwen was my grandmother?" I ask. "Mom said my grandmother's name was Margaret."

"Margaret Gwen," says Aunt Emma. "But she was always called Gwen. That's all I've ever heard your uncles call her."

"Mom told me she was Margaret," I insist.

There's a silence. Then Aunt Emma sighs. "Yes, well. I suppose your mother just knew from the legal papers, and they wouldn't have told what your grandmother was called."

Then, before I know what she's going to do, Aunt Emma pulls me to her in a hug. "Poor kid," she says.

"I am not," I say, stepping back. "Don't call me 'poor kid.' I am not poor."

"I didn't mean you are, Mandy," says Aunt Emma.

"Then what?"

Aunt Emma steps away also. "I guess that I feel sorry for Gwen, and for your mother."

"You didn't know my mother." I'm furious that Emma thinks it's OK to pity her.

"Of course not," Emma says. "You're right."

In my room I try to bring to a standstill the turning pieces of what I've learned. Try to make them into a new picture.

I go to the dressing table, find Mom's photo, move my hand to the picture next to it. Remember how it was blurred and shadowy and that, really, the only detail was a young man's grin. "So, if you're my grandfather, and if Gwen was my grandmother, then maybe you're Paul."

I imagine Paul in an airman's jacket. Imagine him grinning. Bring that together with what I remember of the picture I am holding and know I can make the two faces merge.

But it's too uneasy a shift to make, and I try to put it out of my mind. Gwen and Paul, my *grandparents*—suddenly they're real and I don't think I want them to be. I shouldn't know what my grandparents were like when they were dating.

I make sure the window is closed tight, push the lace curtains back, and catch them behind hooks on the sides of the window frames.

And what's more, I want to be angry with Gwen, tell her I don't want to see her again. Tell her that if she didn't want to have anything to do with my mom, then I don't want to have anything to do with her. But what I really feel is bewildered. I want to ask what happened, why she did it. But not today.

I press my forehead against the cold glass. I don't want to hear more, not today.

I get out homework, but after a few minutes I put it away again. I can't do schoolwork, not through hot tears.

I pick out what I'll wear in the morning.

Then I turn on my notetaker. It's equipment that rehab got for me, sort of like a laptop computer only it's really a combination word processor and calculator with speech, and it has a typewriter keyboard. I type in *Christmas List,* and hit the key for audio feedback.

"Christmas list," a voice says.

But I can't get Gwen out of my thoughts. She's with me, a grief someplace inside that I don't know how to make go away.

I can't get away from Christmas, either, not with every place I go smelling of Christmas trees and with radio stations playing Christmas music and everybody talking about gifts. Everybody.

"Forget the presents," I want to tell people, but they'll think I mean that Christmas isn't about gifts, it's about Jesus, and that's not what I mean at all. What I mean is that gifts are a burden, and I dread gift-giving times.

Like Tuesday, at lunch. I'm sitting with Hannah's group, thinking partly about Gwen, partly about the sandwich I'm trying to eat neatly. Trying to close my ears to the cafeteria racket, which is impossible to sort into anything meaningful.

Suddenly I hear Charla's voice cutting through the noise. "I've gotten all your gifts, and they're all the same thing."

I freeze in my seat, wishing I was somewhere else. It's like hearing people talk about a party you haven't been asked to, or phone calls you haven't been part of.

"Have you all bought your presents for me?" Charla says, with a little giggle to show she knows she shouldn't ask.

Hannah says, "Not yet," and the others answer.

I pull my arms in miserably, hating gift exchanges.

I take a tough piece of chicken from my sandwich, try to look like I'm not paying attention to everybody around me talking about how they're going to shop for each other.

Then Charla says, "Mandy, what about you?"

I'm slow realizing she means I'm being included.

It's Hannah who answers. "Mandy's going shopping with me."

chapter 9

I KEEP my window closed now, the curtains bunched behind their hooks.

Before, seeing Gwen really was like reading a book. I wanted things to turn out OK, but if they didn't it wouldn't matter, not really.

Now, knowing she is my grandmother, what happens does matter. I'm afraid to see it, afraid for her and for me.

So I keep the closed window and still curtains between us. I concentrate on being Mandy, which is difficult enough.

School's getting harder, and my teachers seem to think I should be able to keep up with all the other kids. I am not going to tell them that twenty minutes of home-work for the others means at least an hour for me.

More like two hours in English, where the teacher gives notes nonstop. Sometimes I spend my whole homework time going back and forth on tapes, trying to find something she's said.

No geography, anyway.

One morning the first week in December the geography teacher meets me at the door. "Mandy," he says, "you've been re-scheduled and won't be in my class any longer."

He sounds so satisfied, it's all I can do to hold in my anger. Don't hold it in.

"You, you . . ." I'm almost sputtering with the effort it takes not to call him some aw-ful name, not to use words I don't want anyone to know I know, not to let on I care. "I was keeping up!"

A hand rests on my shoulder, just long enough to get my attention. "Mandy?" says a man's voice. "I hear you could teach this class." Somehow I know he's really saying it to the geography teacher.

The man turns out to be an orientation

and mobility instructor named Mr. Burkhart. For the next couple of months I'll be seeing him twice a week during third period and having study hall the rest of the time. "O & M," he says, "that's the name of the game."

He's nice and kind of jokey-loud, and pretty soon I'm thinking of him as the Great Om. I learn more in an hour from him than I can pick up on my own in days.

Big stuff, like how to identify street intersections, deal with traffic, ask people for directions when they don't have a clue where north and south are.

He has me practice things like trailing, following a wall, listening for the water fountain outside the library.

"Snap your fingers, Mandy," Mr. Burkhart says, and I hear how the sound changes as we pass by an open doorway.

He asks questions like "Mandy, how do you search for something you've dropped?"

The answer is very carefully, curved fingers ready to pull back at the first touch of danger, or before I break whatever I'm looking for.

"Mandy," he says, "what are you going to

do when you're all alone in a strange place and you don't have your cane?"

He won't settle for "sit down and cry," and instead makes me learn how to feel my way forward, one arm protecting my face, a hand in front of my lower body.

The Great Om. My guide to moving through space.

He says not to try to remember it all, but after he leaves I put as much as I can think of into my tape recorder. The things he teaches, they're not like math or history lessons. I *do* have to remember them all.

So, yeah, school's getting harder.

And at home Gabriel keeps asking if I've shopped for Aunt Emma yet. Sooner or later I'm going to have to tell him I don't know what to buy. And I will feel so dumb, but it's a big thing, to get it right.

Also, I've got my dress for the dance Friday and I don't know what I look like in it, although Aunt Emma tries to tell me when I put it on so she can mark how much to take up the hem.

"The copper matches the highlights in your hair, Mandy," she says. "A nice fit— you've got a sweet figure."

Uncle Gabriel asks, "Isn't it a little old for her?"

"Nonsense," says Aunt Emma. "She's a young lady."

It's the lowest-cut thing I've ever owned, except a swimsuit, and Aunt Emma says I'm a lady in it. I hope, somewhere, Mom's laughing.

On dance night Hannah picks me up, the way we planned. We get Ryan and go last to Ted's.

"Let's all go in," Hannah says before I have to ask where the door is. Also, this way I can leave my cane in the car, and that's been worrying me. I want Ted to see me in my new dress, without it.

Ted's parents are just like Aunt Emma was after the football game, acting like this date is Ted going on a world cruise. His mother takes so many pictures she has to change film, and his dad offers us cookies. Then his mother fusses over my dress and Hannah's and fixes and refixes Ted's tie.

"I'm sorry about that," says Ted as we walk to the car. He sounds absolutely, miserably embarrassed, which is one way I've never heard him sound before.

"Parents," says Ryan, like it's no big deal. "They're all like that."

I barely hear Hannah's quiet, "No, they're not."

The dance is fantastic.

Whatever worry Ted had about not hearing the music, I realize right away it's not going to be a problem. The DJ has the volume up loud enough to feel, and certainly loud enough to blast its way past Ted's ears.

And I know I can dance. I always have been able to, even if it used to be alone, in front of a mirror.

There's a moment when Ted shouts in my ear, "Want to try?" that I'd chicken out if I could. But he's pulling me into an empty spot, and I'm moving, little movements, and then bigger and bigger.

Dancing in the dark is like nothing I've ever done before. Sometimes I brush against Ted, or get bumped by somebody else, but even that feels good. I dance, and the music goes on and on, and I can imagine what everything looks like with me in the middle of it all.

Me, Mandy, in the middle of it all.

I'm having such a good time it's a shock when the music stops.

"Mandy," says Ted, and his voice seems both unsure and proud, "you're beautiful."

No one's ever told me that before.

When the music starts back up, Ted has to ask, "Are you ready?" because I'm still standing there thinking about what he said.

I find the beat. "Ready," I answer.

We're out there for dance after dance, until suddenly it's time for the DJ to take a break and Hannah and Ryan are next to us. "Come on," Hannah says, "let's get in line for pictures."

And while we're waiting she whispers, "Where'd you learn to dance like that? Mandy, you're good."

"How was the dance?" Emma asks. She and both uncles have waited up.

"Wonderful," I say.

The room is warm from how happy they are for me.

They've got the TV on, and I sit down next to Emma on the sofa. She puts an arm around me, pulls my head to her shoulder. "A good time, huh?"

Her shoulder is bony and soft at once. I guess it won't hurt to be held, a little while.

Then, upstairs, I find someone has gotten my room ready for me. My bed is turned down, my window open, the lace curtains down from their hooks.

I don't want to be pulled out there, not now, not when, for once, things are close to perfect.

But I hear a voice calling, Gwen's mother calling her, and I can't shut it out. I'm drawn, slow and unwilling, into Gwen's world. Slow like a spoon being pulled from honey. Past limp curtains that hang summer still even though it's December, I'm pulled into a syrup night.

I feel as though I'm somersaulting slowly through the thick night into a motionless day.

Turning in slow motion to see my room. Its painted pink walls bounce sunlight so bright it hurts my eyes. A clutter of things that aren't mine—bobby pins and nail polish and movie magazines—cover the dressing table.

It is a day that feels 110 degrees, and Gwen is stretched out on the bed, looking too hot to move. I can feel the uncertainty in her, knotting her belly. . . .

"Gwen, GwwennnNNN . . . I need you!"

Gwen rolled onto her stomach. If she didn't answer, maybe her mother wouldn't come for her. Wouldn't need her enough to climb all those stairs to come get her.

Hot. It seemed like the hottest August ever.

She pulled the back of her shirt out of her shorts and waited for the fan to come around and dry her back. Rolled over and bared her front. Felt the sweat evaporate so fast her stomach chilled into goose bumps even while the rest of her poured more sweat.

She covered her ears against her mother's footsteps coming up the attic stairs.

"Gwen, didn't you hear me . . . Gwen! Pull down your clothes and get off that bed. That's no place to be in the middle of the day, anyway, and you without a shred of modesty. I don't know what . . ."

"Gwen, why didn't you . . ."

"Gwen, how many times have I told you . . ."

"I'm coming, Mama," said Gwen, sitting up as if she was. But when her mother's footsteps went away, Gwen dropped back. Remembered . . .

"Gwen, come away with me," Paul had said, his face sweaty against hers. "Gwen, I love you."

And Gwen had wondered if she would ever know him well enough to say, "You were the first person to tell me that." Probably not, he'd think she was saying he was the first boy. How do you tell someone you're from a house where nobody says "I love you"?

"Gwen," he'd said, "please come with me."

And she'd known he'd meant to Louisiana, where they'd find someone who'd not push questions about how old she was and who'd marry them. Marry them, and when Paul left to join the Air Force, his going wouldn't be an end—they'd be married.

"OK," she'd said. It had seemed so much better than staying home and snapping beans forever in the hot summer.

She'd made up a story for her mother about visiting a girlfriend and she'd gone off with Paul.

Come back with Paul three days later, in time for him to report for induction. "I'll send for you as soon as I can," he'd promised.

Come home alone and told her mother she'd had an all right visit with her girlfriend.

And now the afternoons were hotter than ever, and she had to tear up Paul's letters once she read them because they started, "Dear Wife."

Dear God, fifteen. What had she done?

Her mother was again at the foot of the stairs. "Gwen, I want you downstairs *now*, and working . . ."

chapter 10

SATURDAY MORNING I sleep late and stay in bed even later, my thoughts going back and forth between Gwen and the dance.

Gwen, secretly married at fifteen?

Me, a success at a dance? I run my fingers along my face and wonder if it has changed from the way I remember. Am I really beautiful, like Ted said?

I hear Emma and Gabriel in the hall beneath the attic stairs. Gabriel's heavy footsteps come partway up to my door, but I hold my breath and keep perfectly still. He goes back down, says, "I think she's still asleep, Emma."

"Let her be," Emma answers. "I used to sleep in after a dance, too."

And a moment later I hear Emma laugh. "Put me down, silly. I've too much to do for dancing in the middle of the day."

But Gabriel's singing something, and his footsteps are in three-beat time. And then he switches to another song, and it's one my mother used to like.

Mom . . . I remember how she'd hum it. Her body wouldn't really move, but she'd seem like she was swaying, lost in a still waltz.

I remember her sitting in front of her makeup mirror, humming, frowning a bit because she was trying to match a magazine picture. The lipstick was dark stuff, deep red.

"It says you've got to respect your contrasts," Mom said.

Mom must have been about forty then. The deep color made her look even older, but I didn't want to tell her.

It was Christmas morning, the Christmas morning we were living in Florida, and we didn't either one of us have anything to do. I'd given her a leather key case with her name, Karen, stamped on it, and she'd gotten me a necklace with a silver flamingo, but we'd finished opening those in about five minutes and the hours had stretched out since.

Mom leaned closer to the mirror, seemed to decide she was done and she wasn't going to stay in the apartment any longer. "Come on, kid," she said, "let's join America."

So we'd gone out to join America, only America had closed down. The mall was shut, the drugstore, even the kosher deli was shut.

We'd driven to the beach and walked along it, with the old people who were walking two by two, and I thought they were having a lonely Christmas, also.

I'm still in bed, thinking about my mother and about Gwen, when the doorbell rings. I hear Uncle Abe calling, "I'll get it."

A minute more and Hannah's in my room.

"I guess I should have phoned first," she says.

"I wasn't really sleeping."

I wonder if I should tell Hannah what

Gwen has done. It would be fair—Gwen's our secret that we share. But . . . my grandmother, married at fifteen? Such a thing wouldn't happen in Hannah's family, and I don't want her to look down on me.

Besides, it's another personal thing, personal to Gwen, I mean. It wouldn't feel right to expose her like that.

Then I realize Hannah's trying to tell me something.

". . . aren't getting along," she's saying. "They whispered all night, mean whispers, and this morning Dad said he'd be gone for a few days. Mom looked like she'd been crying."

"Everybody fights," I say, the first thing that comes to mind. Actually, I don't have the faintest idea if that's true. I haven't heard Gabriel and Emma fight, and they're the only couple I've ever lived with.

But I've said what Hannah wants to hear, and soon she's rummaging through my dresser, looking for shorts.

"It's practically summer outside," she says. Her voice is too bright, and I know she's already regretting telling me about her folks. "It really is a lot warmer than usual.

Really warm for December. Maybe we can even get tans."

"In December? In the morning?"

"It's afternoon. Didn't you know?"

Hannah's like a cat, moving about my room. I can feel the energy coming off her, the way you can feel it come off the big caged cats at a zoo.

"Don't you ever feel like breaking out?" she asks. "I feel like I can't breathe in here."

Now she's dragging me downstairs, saying, "Let's sleep outside tonight. You ever sleep outside, Mandy?"

"Outside?" I echo, feeling dumb but not sure I know what she means.

"In a tent?"

We find Emma sorting wrapping paper. She says, "Certainly you can't sleep outside. It's December."

But Hannah promises we'll keep warm and the weather forecast is good, and I hear myself saying, "Please, Aunt Emma."

So while I'm getting dressed, Hannah helps Uncle Gabriel get an old tent from the barn, a pup tent from his army days, he says. They set it up by the side of the house.

Hannah and I spend the rest of the afternoon hauling stuff out to it, like we're preparing a room to move into. We run an extension cord so we can plug in my CD player. Get a cooler from the pantry and fill it with ice and sodas. Take out blankets and pillows and two big feather comforters.

I'm blowing up an air mattress, listening to hear if air's escaping out any holes, when it comes to me that I'm going to be outside at night, out where Gwen's and the others' voices have come from.

As though Hannah and my aunt have each caught some small part of my thoughts, Hannah says she wishes we had her Ouija board, and Emma asks, "Are you sure you girls won't be scared?"

Gabriel reassures her. "We'll keep our bedroom window open. The girls can call if they need anything."

We go out to stay about nine o'clock, and Hannah tells me it's a dark night, without any moon.

"Hang on to me, Mandy," she says, "I've got the flashlight." Then we start giggling because that's crazy, the dark is no different for me.

We settle in, and the temperature's dropped enough that the blankets feel good. About the time Hannah's saying we should have got hot chocolate instead of cold drinks, Aunt Emma comes out.

"I've brought you girls a couple of my flannel nightgowns," she says. "I don't want either of you getting sick this close to Christmas."

And after she leaves we pull them on over our T-shirts and underpants.

And maybe it's that, being out of the house in mainly underwear, that makes this night seem wild and wicked and not a night to just let end.

"You sleepy, Hannah?" I ask.

"No."

"I wish we could do something, go some-place."

A car drives by on the road and slows down.

"Mandy," says Hannah. "The lights picked up our tent."

She pauses, draws in her breath, whispers, "What if it's a kidnapper? Or a serial killer?" Hannah is faking fright, and I realize she feels the excitement in this night the way I do.

"Hannah, save me. I'm too young to die," I say, trying to sound terrified.

Hannah switches to her phony voice, the one she used with the Ouija board. "It might be," she says, spacing her words, "the Texas ax murderer. The one who likes young girls!"

She grabs me so fast I scream before I can help it, and she says, "Shush!"

"You two all right down there?" Emma calls.

"We're fine, thank you," Hannah calls back.

I hear her move to the foot of the tent and undo a couple of snaps.

"Mandy," she says, and this time her voice really is a bit shaky, "the car's backing up." Then, and her voice is altogether different, "Mandy, I think it's Ted's car . . . It *is*."

She's gripping my arm and undoing the rest of the snaps. "Be quiet," she says and pulls me, almost running, toward the street.

Almost running, and it feels like flying;

I'm moving fast along the lawn in Aunt Emma's nightgown. My bare feet pound on winter-dry cold grass, pound down on stinging thistles, and cool air blows up my legs. Hannah says, "Careful," just as we bump up against Ted's car.

"You OK, Mandy?" It's Ryan's voice. There's a pause and then he adds, "Pretty sexy clothes."

"You like?" asks Hannah.

Ted ignores the two of them. "You shouldn't be barefoot, Mandy. You could step on a piece of glass or something." He must realize how fussy he sounds. "You want to go into town for something to eat?"

"Now?" Hannah asks. "We can't . . ."

"Why not?" I hear myself saying, and then I'm getting in the front seat next to Ted, and Hannah's in the back with Ryan.

And for an hour we drive around town, ducking every time we meet another car because Hannah and I are in Aunt Emma's nightgowns.

Except at the hamburger place, where we get french fries and Hannah knows the girl at the drive-in window. "Sit up and say something, Mandy," she whispers. "We'll pretend we're going to a costume party."

And then, after all that hiding, we're driving along listening to the radio when suddenly Hannah says, "Ted, stop."

She reaches past me to turn the music up loud, and in another minute all four of us are out in the middle of the road, dancing. Dancing in the headlights of Ted's car, lights that shine through my eyelids when I turn toward them.

Cars go past and everyone honks, and the guys are laughing as hard as we are.

Then Ted says, "That's a police cruiser," and we scramble back inside his car.

We're sitting in the car's four corners, trying to act like we haven't been doing anything unusual, when the patrolman comes to the window. He swings his flashlight around; I see the light when it crosses my eyes.

"You kids OK?" His voice gets louder, I guess at some indication from Ted. "Everything all right here?"

"Yes, sir," says Ted.

But the patrolman says, "Girls?" and waits until both Hannah and I answer.

"Then you better get on home and get dressed," he says.

"Yes, sir," says Ted again, and then, once we're driving, we laugh and laugh like we're going to laugh forever. I say, "Ted, he meant us, Hannah and I should get dressed."

"How do you know?" Ryan asks, and the four of us about die laughing, Ryan the hardest, and Hannah tells Ted to watch the road.

chapter 11

H ANNAH AND I wake up in the
tent, sometime in the middle of the night.
It's cold and damp, and I say, "Hannah, let's
go up to my room." We go inside, climb into
my big double bed, which is chilly, too, until the sheets warm.

And then we don't wake up again until
Aunt Emma's at the steps, calling that if
we're not downstairs within the hour we'll
miss lunch.

"I can't believe we did that, go to town in
nightgowns," Hannah says.

"Me either."

"My mom would kill me."

"Aunt Emma, too," I say, even though I

don't think she would. "I had fun last night."

"Me, too." Hannah pauses, and I get the idea she's choosing her next words carefully. "Mandy, don't take this wrong and get all huffy, but I want you to know I really admire you." Her voice takes on a raw edge, like she's suddenly close to tears. "I mean, whatever happens, you just kind of charge forward and deal with it, and I'm not always so good at that."

There's no way I can imagine she's joking because her voice tells me she's not, and I'm too stunned to answer quickly enough.

Hannah turns over, and when she speaks again the rawness is gone. "I guess if my folks get a divorce my brother and I will stay with Mom. Dad will probably get us on weekends."

"Is that what you want?"

"That's how it's usually done," she says. "Want doesn't come into it."

"Want doesn't come into it." Gwen's mother's words, and hearing Hannah say them makes the skin on my arms tighten into goose bumps.

Hannah asks, "Should I pull up another blanket? You shivered."

"No," and I'm thinking back, trying to remember if I'd told her those words. Maybe they're Texas words, I think, and everyone says them.

Hannah stays with me through the afternoon, even though she listens every time the phone rings, like she's hoping it's for her. We both know things must be really weird at her house if her mother's not calling her to come home.

Hannah opens my bedroom window. "Mandy, have you seen Gwen anymore?"

"No," I say, guilty because I'm lying but still not wanting to tell her about the last time.

"Come try," Hannah urges until I stand next to her. "Call," she says, insistent in a way that's not like her.

"Gwen," I yell, feeling stupid, "Gwen."

I tell Hannah, "This isn't how it works."

"You mean Gwen won't let me see her," Hannah says, jerking me inside and pulling down the window.

Pulling it down on the voice in the wind.

She hasn't heard, but I have. Little Abe is calling Gwen.

In the evening, when I'm alone again, I go back to the window. To reach out to Gwen, or to wait for her to let me go to her. I've stopped knowing which way it is.

I find her summer has turned into a chill December, and her house has become a house of careful, small moments. . . .

Gwen wandered through the rooms, touching this, looking at that, as if she was trying to memorize things.

Abe came in from outside, dropping his coat in the hall.

"Want to go play a game?" he asked.

Gwen swooped him up and hugged him so tightly he said, "Let me down, you're hurting."

Then she went up to the attic, to her room. She ran her hand along a shell pink wall and starched lace curtain. Looked across the stretching fields, already rented out now that her father was gone.

She opened a drawer and wondered what she should take.

"You're leaving, aren't you?" Her mother's voice at the doorway made her jump. "I thought so."

"How did you know?"

"Gwen, please. It can't be so bad here that you have to run away."

"There's not anything bad, Mama," Gwen said. "It's just that . . ."

"Then why?" her mother asked, but she didn't wait for an answer. She shook her head as though she had already decided arguing was useless. "Well, I can't stop you, but I won't take you back, either."

Gwen spent the next long hours by herself, waiting for evening, for Paul. He'd written that he'd found a room for her just off base, that he was using his first real leave to come get her. Gwen had planned to go off with him and then write, but somehow her mother had guessed.

Her mother came up to the attic just once more. "I hope you'll get married?"

"We already are," Gwen said.

Her mother made a strangled sound,

more like a snort than anything. "Here, then," and she thrust one of her own nightgowns into Gwen's hands. "You can't go to your husband in pajamas."

When Paul's car sounded in the drive, Gwen grabbed her suitcase and ran down all the stairs and out to meet him. And then, for all her hurrying, she looked back. Looked back at an empty porch and nobody waving good-bye.

Her mother's nightgown was on top of everything, in her suitcase.

Ted has started picking me up on his way to school. It's not far out of his way.

He honks and I go out to his car, a vehicle that he is very proud of. He got it right after he got his license, he told me, because the bus doesn't go near his house and his mother wanted to stop driving.

"His parents," Aunt Emma said, "think the sun rises and sets on that boy. If he wanted his own airplane, they'd find a way to give it to him."

This morning I'm only halfway to his car when he calls, "Mandy, come here and hold out your hands. Together and carefully."

He puts something soft and warm and incredibly light in my palms. "A baby possum," he says. "I found it by the road."

"Alone?"

"A big one was nearby, run over. I think it was this one's mother."

The baby is so small I can almost hold it in one palm, and I'm terrified I'll hurt it. "Take it, Ted," I say, "before I drop it."

"You won't. You can raise it."

"Me? You found it. Him. Her. Whatever."

But even as I talk, groping for a joke, my insides are thumping over because I want so much to care for the little thing. I'm wishing I dared trust it to one hand. I want the other free to stroke it, and find the top of its head, and how its tail feels.

At the same time, I'm panicky.

"I don't know anything about taking care of an animal," I say. "I've never had a pet. What do you feed it?"

"It's a baby, Mandy." Ted sounds exasperated, but he's laughing, too. "Milk, of course."

"And Aunt Emma probably won't let me keep it. If she wanted a pet, she'd have a cat or a dog."

"Why don't you ask?"

I pull back one hand just a little, begin to explore the hairless tip of its tail with my finger. A low growl and hiss make me wonder if I'm going to get bitten. Then I realize probably it's the baby that's frightened.

I leave the opossum with Ted and go in the house to find Aunt Emma. I was right about her not wanting a pet. "Keeping a wild animal is probably not even legal," she says. "I'll call the shelter and see what they say to do."

I won't beg. It's something I've never done and I'm not going to begin now. I turn, walk partway down the hall.

And turn again and go back.

"Please, Aunt Emma. Just until it can go out on its own?"

"Mandy . . ."

"Please?"

There's a long silent moment, a moment in which I swear to myself that if Aunt Emma says no I won't ever ask her for anything again. Won't ever ask anyone for anything. I shrug and start to say, "Never mind."

"I guess," she says, "we could try feeding

it some of the milk replacer your uncles keep on hand for calving. I should have an eyedropper somewhere."

Then she catches my arm as Ted and I are leaving. "Mandy, it probably won't live, you know. Wild things often don't."

I'd like to say it doesn't matter, but I can't. "Please don't let it die, Aunt Emma," I say. "Please, please don't."

Ted, on the drive to school, is absolutely delighted with himself, all out of proportion to saving an orphaned opossum.

At school Hannah's lining up my day, telling me we should go shopping in the afternoon.

I tell her I can't. I have to get home to the opossum.

Besides, I wish Hannah would understand that I don't want her help shopping. Finding the right presents for Aunt Emma and the uncles is something I should be able to do by myself.

The school halls are even more noisy than usual, and at lunch the cafeteria is thundering with band instruments playing a preview of a holiday concert. I can't hear what anybody is saying, can't even hear voices well enough to know who's sitting where.

"I'm leaving," I shout, to whoever's listening. I get up, only where I thought there was a space there's not and I knock a tray crashing to the floor. I reach down, touch something cold and wet, wonder how to clean up.

Someone says, "I'll get it."

I sink back into my chair. For a moment everything—the tray, all the noise—it's more than I can deal with.

"Hey," somebody yells in my ear, "you're complaining about the food?" I recognize Ryan's voice. He's trying to make me feel better.

Then Hannah's with me, and we're walking outside toward the building where the resource room is.

"I don't know what happened," I begin. I realize I owe Hannah some sort of explanation, but I'm just too tired and overwhelmed to make it. The opossum, Aunt Emma giving in to me, those blasted presents I don't know what to do about . . . This day feels like it's been thirty hours long.

"Sometimes I just want to get away from everything."

"Me too," says Hannah.

In Ms. Z.'s room I slump into a seat, and for once nobody comes and asks me if I need help. I must sit there twenty or thirty minutes, listening to the quiet click and chunk of keyboards and printers, to the hum of machinery fans, to the murmur of one of the boys reading under his breath. Slowly things calm down inside me, until I'm finally ready to get to work.

I go to my computer and begin a file for a paper I'm writing for English. The assignment is to capture an instant using sensory detail. I'm doing mine on an early summer morning, as far from Christmas as I can get.

It's pretty boring stuff, how the sunrise looked through the back window of the car the summer Mom and I drove west. How the sky went clear down to the earth. How empty the road was, empty as we were because we hadn't stopped for breakfast yet, empty like I always felt when we'd left one place and hadn't yet found the next.

I hear someone come up behind me. Ms. Z. says, "You make it seem real."

"It's just what I remember," I say.

"Being able to remember details is a gift."

And then she goes away and Ted takes her place. He must have been watching us, reading our lips, because he says, "I heard the ocean once, in a seashell. When I was little, before my hearing got so bad. But I don't have words for the sound."

I know what he's saying, that he wishes he could put sounds on paper, to keep them.

The way I wish I could know for sure I won't ever forget the sky, or the color of an empty road.

"I hope Ms. Z.'s right," I say, "about me having a gift for remembering. Because sometimes I wake up and everything is black, and for an awful time I wonder if I've forgotten how it was, what things looked like."

"Like the sun," says Ted. "Like the sun through the car window. You won't, Mandy."

I shrug. How can he know?

chapter 12

, , ,
, ,
,

Emma's waiting for me on the front lawn when I get home. She tells me right away that the opossum is alive. "Cute little thing," she says. "And hungry! He's been eating all day, eating and sleeping."

Emma's been busy, made some phone calls, bought some stuff that is supposed to be better than the cow milk replacer. "Not," she says, "that he doesn't seem just as happy eating bugs."

She leads me to where she's got him in a big carton on the front porch. The opossum's half hidden in a pile of leaves in one corner, and Emma tells me he moved them there himself.

"I'll sit out here with him awhile," I say. Then, as she goes inside, I add, "Thank you, Aunt Emma."

"You're welcome," she says, and she sounds enormously pleased.

The uncles have missed all this, the opossum, I mean, because they've been gone since before dawn to a stock show. Now their car turns in the drive. Uncle Gabriel calls to me that he's going out to the barn and will be along in a while, and Abe comes up the steps.

"What have you got there?" he asks.

"An opossum. An orphan."

"It's pretty big," he says. "Probably born in September and about ready to go out on its own."

"I'd wondered why there would be a baby now, instead of spring."

"Possums have young different times of the year," Abe says. "Carry them around in pouches like kangaroos until they grow a decent size. When they're born they're about the size of my thumbnail."

126

The one I'm holding suddenly seems a lot bigger, as I try to picture him just a bit bigger than my thumbnail. Without warning he wraps his tail around my finger and drops to my lap. The tail, unwrapping itself, tickles. "I think this one's going to be a circus performer."

I say that and a memory clicks in sharp, clicks in about circuses. Without taking time to think I say, "You used to have a circus, didn't you? When you were little? A pill bug circus?"

I hear Abe catch his breath, then the silence of him holding it, like he can't breathe. Then his harsh, "What makes you say that?"

And I'm frightened to tell him, frightened and feeling that I'm at the edge of something terribly sad.

"Oh," I say, "I don't know. I guess I was just thinking most kids like bugs."

This night there's no calling when I first lean out the window. I lean out farther and wait a long time, wait in air cold and heavy. And then I hear the child's thin, crying voice, little Abe's voice. . . .

"Gwen, Gwen? Please, Gwenny, come back."

"I miss Gwen," Abe said. "Will she ever come back?" He was standing close by his mother, as if standing so close would make her answer.

"Gwen's best forgotten," she said. "Go play."

But after he went outside, she stepped to the secretary, took an envelope off the top. She pulled out a letter and read over it quickly, as if she was looking again at something she'd already memorized. Pressed her lips together. Murmured, "Just what do you expect from me?"

She tore the letter three times across and three times down, and after that she tore up the envelope. "I told you I wouldn't have you back."

Then she sat in a rocker, closed her eyes, and murmured, "I did what was right, didn't I? Told you the consequences if you left?"

After a while she went to the wastebasket, pulled out the pieces of paper, and tried to fit the envelope back together. Tried, and couldn't, and gave up.

It's Saturday again. Aunt Emma is standing at the kitchen table, wiring pine boughs into a wreath. The uncles have put a Christmas tree up in the living room, and the boughs are what they cut off the bottom.

"They smell so good," I say, picking one up. Sap sticks to my fingers and I try to roll it off. The wonder is the boughs can be smelled at all among all the other smells. Aunt Emma has spiced cider heating on the stove and cookies baking. Ginger and cinnamon and apple run into the cool air that comes from a window she's cracked open, air that smells just a little of damp earth and cows and hay.

"Aunt Emma," I start, and then don't know quite what I want to say. That this is like a book, maybe, or a TV family. "Aunt Emma," I say, "you've made this house nice."

"It's you that's made it nice, Mandy. You can't imagine what pleasure you're giving your uncles and me."

Then she hugs me. Something scratchy, a piece of pine branch caught on her dress maybe, tickles my neck, and her cheek next to mine feels floury.

I start to pull away, but then I think, why? And so I give her a little hug back. I'm not sure what to do with my arms, which makes the whole thing clumsy, but I guess it's an OK hug. Emma says, "How about pouring us some cider?" and her voice tells me how pleased she is.

I take down two mugs and position them on the counter, where they'll be easy to find after I pick up the saucepan. I hear wire being clipped, so I know my aunt has returned to her wreath making. She's not even watching me, is she? She knows that I can do this. It's silly, I guess, but I feel quite proud of myself.

I'm proud of Aunt Emma, too. I know it was hard for her the day my caseworker said sooner or later I'd have to learn to cook for myself and it might as well be sooner.

"But it's so easy to get burned," Aunt Emma had protested. "And there are sharp knives, and . . ."

And we'd all gone out into the kitchen

and the caseworker had marked the stove dials with a 3-D marker. "One line at twelve o'clock for *off*, Mandy, two lines at three o'clock for *high*."

And now, thinking about Aunt Emma and me, how we're working together in the kitchen, this leads to another thought. It's one that's tangled, but I like it—a thought that I'm fitting in here.

Me pouring us cider and it not being something to especially notice, that doesn't have anything to do with how well I can get about on my own. It's because I'm family. Doing for each other, it's how a family is.

Or should be.

"Aunt Emma?" I say.

"Yes?"

"Will you answer a question?"

"If I know the answer."

"When Uncle Abe and Uncle Gabriel were little, what was it like here?"

She takes awhile, as though she's searching through details. Finally she says, "They've never talked much about when they were little. But I can imagine."

She shuffles pine boughs before continuing. "The first year we were married, your uncle Gabriel and I, I wanted to buy the most beautiful Christmas tree we could and decorate it with him. But his mother—this was her house, and we were living with her then—said if we had so much money we ought to be able to find a better use for it. She set a scrawny little tree out on a table, put it up one day when nobody was home, like it was just one more job that needed doing."

"Do you think she loved Gabriel and Abe?" I ask.

Aunt Emma blows on the cider I hand her, then sips a bit. "I don't know. I suppose, as much as she was able. I probably shouldn't say, I was just a daughter-in-law, but . . . I always thought she didn't know how to love."

Emma's next words come in a rush. "I wish you could see the old photo albums, Mandy. Her, and her mother, and her mother's mother. Like, like . . ."

"Like coldness passed on?" I ask.

"Exactly," Aunt Emma says, sounding surprised, as if I've shown her something she's never seen before. "Like coldness passed on."

chapter 13

I HEAR the crying outside my bedroom window, hear it even though I stay in bed, try to smother my ears with covers.

I hear the boy's voice, crying for Gwen.

I hear Gwen's voice from a far distance, awful cries . . .

"Paul, stop falling. Please God, don't let him, don't . . . Paulllll!"

. . . Gwen? . . .

"How can he be dead? What do I do now?"

Monday is Big-Little Day at school, something done around here for enough years that no one thinks the name is funny. All the second graders in the district spend the morning in high school, parceled out one-on-one to sophomores and juniors.

"I think they're supposed to see how much they have to look forward to," Hannah tells me when I ask why.

Ted, who is standing with us, says, "Which we'll demonstrate by coloring Santa pictures, serving snacks in every class, and limiting the academics to rented videos."

"Not really," I say.

"Really," they answer in unison.

"What?" Ted adds. "You expected truth in advertising from a school district?"

Anyway, today I am to personally convince Robert Carlo, who is seven years old and wants to be called by his whole name, that high school is a great place to be.

Robert Carlo is more interested in me than in high school.

"I've never met a blind person before," he says.

"We go to math first," I tell him. "I bet we have juice and something to eat and watch a movie."

"How do you find the room?"

"With my cane."

"How does your cane tell you?"

"It's got an electronic elf inside that sends radio wave messages to my brain. In code."

There's a long pause while Robert Carlo considers the possibility. I laugh.

"My math class is around the first corner from where we are now, then six doors down. I use my cane to count the doors."

Wrong thing to tell Robert Carlo. "You ever lose count?" he asks as we walk. "Two, six, nine. Can you add forty-three, thirteen, and a hundred and fifty-five?" he jabbers. "Eight, eleven, one million . . ."

Charla goes by. "He's my next-door neighbor," she says. "You've got my sympathy."

We reach a second corner and I realize we've missed the room. "We have to go back," I say. "This time, Robert Carlo, shut up."

A small, grimy-feeling hand slips into mine, and a moment later I hear, "Mandy? I'm sorry."

Robert Carlo eats doughnuts and asks questions nonstop. Fortunately, the TV volume is so loud our whispering during the movie doesn't seem to bother anyone.

Robert Carlo wants to know if being blind hurts.

Why I bother to keep my eyes open.

If my fingers get sore when I read braille, and I have to tell him I don't read braille very well yet.

He wants to know if I can see anything at all.

"Light, sometimes, if it's very strong. And once in a great while I feel what color something is."

"No way," he says. "You can't feel color."

And of course he grabs my hand, sticks it on a book, and demands, "What color? Can you feel what color this is?"

"I said, *sometimes.*"

How do I explain what I don't understand myself? How every once in a while I'll touch something and my brain will be flooded with an image of red, or blue, and when I ask I find out that's what color the thing really is?

The movie sound snaps off midsentence. For the first time I am aware that other kids have edged in close to Robert Carlo and me.

A boy who sounds like another second grader asks, "How do you take tests?"

A girl asks, "Do you have to help at home?"

Some snot says, "What could she do?"

"Plenty," I say, I guess a bit snappy. "I set the table, dust, help with feeding the cows. I wash my own clothes, make my bed every morning . . ."

The same kid says, "Your folks must be dictators."

"Right," I tell him. I start to leave it at that and then realize I can't. What if it got back to Aunt Emma and my uncles?

"My folks are not dictators," I say. "They just want me to know how much I can do."

The bell rings but nobody moves. Then Mr. Casie says, "Thank you, Mandy."

Robert Carlo takes possession of my hand again. And a little girl says, "Mandy, you have pretty eyes."

The days are going by quickly, punctuated by feeding times for my opossum. It seems every time I pick him up, he's grown a bit and become a bit more independent. Hannah comes over on Wednesday afternoon. The weather has turned cold and rainy, and we take cookies and soda up to my room, which is the warmest place in the house. I ask Hannah if there's ever snow in Texas for Christmas.

"I suppose, but not often, except maybe in the panhandle," she says. "Not over here, anyway. Mandy, everyone in town seems to know my folks are considering a divorce. Every place I go, people are nice." After a moment she adds, "I hate it that everyone feels sorry for me."

"Welcome to the club."

"Mandy," she says, "I'm scared."

She sighs and then, like she's forgetting the whole subject, gets up and goes to my dressing table. I hear her picking up first one thing, then another.

"Mandy," she says, "tell me again who the man is."

"My grandfather."

"He's so young in the picture. Is he still alive?"

"No," I say, "I never met him. He died years ago, before I was born, even before my mother was born."

"Then why do you have his picture out?"

I answer carefully because I've been thinking about that myself. "I guess because it was important to my mother," I say. "She always kept that picture on her dresser."

I think back, wondering how much to tell Hannah.

Think back to how my mother would look at that picture, sometimes for ten, fifteen minutes without moving. Then she'd tell me, "That's my father, Mandy, your grandfather, wearing his airman's jacket. Did you ever see anyone so proud? I think he must have just learned my mom was going to have me."

I tell Hannah, "That was all my mother had of her father. He died months before she was born."

Hannah says, "I think that's one of the saddest things I ever heard."

I agree. Still, I can't tell Hannah how sometimes I heard my mother crying in the night. How once I found her standing in front of the picture. "You're promising," she was saying, over and over. "You're grinning like you're promising to come back."

Instead I ask, "Hannah, do you mind very much about your folks splitting up?"

"It hasn't happened yet."

"If they do?"

"It's their lives," she says, and her voice has a new hardness.

"Yeah," I say, thinking I should have minded my own business. "There's no point getting upset over other people's lives."

Alone after Hannah's gone home, I go back to the pictures, hold my grandfather's in one hand, my mom's in the other.

I know exactly how my grandfather's picture looks, the image of a young man's face as it was at one moment. I memorized it years ago.

But Mom's photo has ceased being a fixed thing. I hold it and see how she looked, first at one time and then another, Mom in a set number of memories that won't ever be added to. I hunt through them, find how she'd ask me into her room and show me her father's picture.

"Look, babe," she'd say, "he's grinning. I think he knows I'm going to be born and he's saying, 'Chin up, kid. Hit the world running, kid.' He loved me, Mandy. See how he looks?"

And I'd stand there, thinking that even with just a picture, she'd had more of a father than she'd given me.

I guess it wouldn't have hurt me to say, "Yes, I think he must have loved you." But I never did.

I wonder if, like Gwen, my mom is out there, past the dark, living again in some year when she was young. I want to tell her I'm sorry.

It's the middle of the night, and I'm having trouble sleeping. I pull the covers close. Should I open the window? Hold a piece of lace curtain to my face, smell the faint bleach, the fainter dust?

I tumble, roughly . . . I hear Gwen's voice . . .

Gwen, Gwen . . . Stop screaming, Gwen . . .

"I saw a bird. I couldn't make it keep flying."

And?

"He was fast, falling fast, and his brown feathers were covered with oil and fire. He screeched with wind and terror."

You could hear him?

"His mouth cawed open and he crossed the sky, between me and the plane, he crossed the sun and came cartwheeling down."

The bird?

"Paul."

You saw him?

"Mandy, I wish I could give you my eyes."

Aunt Emma is shaking me, and I hear the uncles in the doorway.

"Mandy, wake up," Emma's saying. "Mandy, you're having a nightmare."

But I know I'm not, and I say, "No, it was Gwen. She was seeing Paul die. He was cartwheeling, down and down."

And then Aunt Emma squeezes my arm so hard it hurts and I jerk the rest of the way awake. "Is that what happened?" I ask. "Did Gwen see her husband die?"

It's Uncle Gabriel who answers. "We never heard," he says. "She never wrote home after she left."

I hear Abe's footsteps; he's going slowly down the stairs like an old man.

Aunt Emma asks, "Do you often think about Gwen?"

And, maybe because it's the middle of the night, I say, "Sometimes I can see everything going on, like I was there, when she was my age."

I wait for them to tell me I'm imagining things, but they don't.

Aunt Emma says, "There have been stranger things."

And Gabriel says, "I'd like to think Gwen knows you, Mandy. She'd be proud."

Only Uncle Abe is upset. I find him alone in the living room the next morning, not doing anything.

"You didn't like me talking about Gwen, did you?" I ask.

I think he shrugs, even though I can't see him.

"Would you please tell me about her?" I ask.

Abe's voice is gruff. He says, "I've got work to do outside. Besides, Gwen went away before I was old enough to remember."

He leaves, and I go to find Aunt Emma. "How old was Uncle Abe when Gwen left home?" I ask.

She does some figuring, subtracting ages and dates, and says she guesses about five or six.

That's what I guessed, too.

Old enough to remember at least a little. But maybe he doesn't want to. Maybe remembering her hurts him too much because he believes she abandoned him.

And then I feel so sorry for him, for them both. I want to go after him and say, "Uncle Abe, Gwen did write, but your mother tore up her letter."

But what good would that do? He probably wouldn't believe me.

Aunt Emma says, "I've often thought how sad it is that Abe can't seem to remember anything about being a child. It's like a part of his life is locked away and he can't get at it."

"Gwen loved her brothers," I say, and I know it with absolute certainty.

"Gabriel realizes that, I think," says Emma. "But I don't know if Abe ever will."

chapter 14

I MIX SOME MILK formula in a bottle and go outside to see if the opossum will come for it, before I have to leave for school. He doesn't stay in his carton anymore, although we leave it on the porch so he can get back in if he wants.

Uncle Abe thinks the sooner the opossum is completely on its own, the better chance it will have of surviving. And I know he's right. When you have to take care of yourself, about the only way to do it is to just get out and start.

Still, I'm glad when I hear the little guy come scrambling up the porch steps. He knocks at my hands and at the plastic bottle before settling down to eat. I don't know if the milk is dessert after food he's gotten on his own or if it's his whole meal.

I wonder if he thinks I'm his mother.

Don't be dumb, Mandy, I tell myself. Opossums can't think.

"Whatever," I say out loud. "I'll take care of you as long as you want." I feel so responsible and . . . so old. Like I really am sort of his mother.

Thinking that makes me think of my own mom. It's the strangest thing, how she seems to be getting younger and younger in my mind.

"It's pretty amazing, how you took care of me," I whisper. I remember back, a lot of things. My mom and me eating hot dogs together at a park, loading a car trunk so full we had to tie it shut, taking in one of her skirts to fit me, trying to make crocuses bloom on a windowsill.

She tried to be a good mother, even though she didn't have any more training at the job than I've got in taking care of opossums. Of course, if she had, maybe sometimes she would have told me she loved me.

She would have known it was something I wanted to hear.

The opossum is scratching my hand, probably hoping for more to eat.

"Sorry," I say. "Too much food could kill you."

I pick him up. "But I guess a little love won't hurt."

I've known as long as I can remember that my mom was put up for adoption when she was born, only the adoption didn't work out and she grew up in a series of foster homes.

All she knew about her real family was what she could guess from a couple of pictures that had arrived in the mail one day, when she was still a kid. They had come with a note that said, "For the little girl."

One was the picture I still have, of her father, taken just before he died. That was written on the back. The other photo was of the house where her mother grew up, this house that I'm living in now.

"Didn't anyone try to find out who sent them?" I once asked.

"Not that I know of," Mom answered. "I was only four or five."

The photo of the house got lost a few years ago, but by then I knew it by heart. Whenever we moved to a new town, I'd watch houses, hoping to find where my grandmother had come from. I had this scene that I'd imagine, how Mom and I would walk up to a door, introduce ourselves . . .

Dumb, but sometimes I'd see Mom checking out houses, too.

I hope she knows I'm living in that very house now, and that it's a nice place.

Hannah's visiting again.

"I hate my parents," she says. "All the fighting, all the time, and they try to be polite about it."

It's late afternoon, and we're walking through the back pasture, the one where there's just cows. The uncles keep the bulls in a different field. It's safe for us to be in this one.

"I'd like to live in the country," Hannah says. She stops to pet a cow that has come over, but as soon as the cow realizes we don't have food, it wanders off. "Other times," Hannah says, "I think I'd like to go away, just run off and disappear forever."

A shiver goes through me. "Don't say that."

"Well, it's what I think," says Hannah. "Sometimes I try to imagine the ways I could go away and not leave a trail that people could follow."

I think, Gwen found a way.

"The bus would be best," Hannah says. "It's hard to lie about your name on a plane ticket because you have to show ID when you check in, and cars are too easy for the police to look for."

"Hannah, I told you, don't talk that way."

But she won't stop. "I'd take a bus going in a direction where all the towns have good-sounding names. And I wouldn't get off until I was at least two states away."

There's no way I can make her understand. Disappearing is not something to joke about. A person doesn't know who she's going to hurt when she goes off and doesn't come back.

If Gwen hadn't disappeared, hadn't gone off and left her baby for strangers to raise, then all those years later my mom wouldn't have started looking for her, and . . . Well, maybe everything would have been different.

$$\text{J } \text{J } \text{J}$$
$$\text{J } \text{J}$$
$$\text{J } \text{J}$$

Mom GOT the idea one evening this past summer. I was fixing a torn swimsuit and she was quietly reading, which was not the way she usually read.

Usually she talked.

"Mandy," she would say, "it says here you can get cancer from the sun," or "California workers get some of the highest wages in the country." Stuff I'd already know, but these things always came as news to Mom.

But this particular evening, Mom wasn't saying a word, and that distracted me so much I asked, "What are you reading about?"

"Nothing," she said, putting down her magazine.

Then five minutes later she said, "Mandy, I'm going to find my mother."

Like, "Mandy, I think I'll get a leather belt for my new slacks."

Mom got up, pulled a package of cookie dough from the freezer, and knocked her knuckles against it. "You think this would thaw pretty quick?"

"Is that what you were reading about, finding parents?"

Mom shoved the dough back. "I guess I don't need the calories. There's a story about how adoption records used to be sealed up, but now they're being opened. More and more people are being reunited with their birth parents."

Poor Mom. I could see the signs—we were going to move again. This time in search of her birth mother.

And she probably expected to find some loving, real-cookie-baking woman delighted to see us. Right. Just the way she'd expected to find sunshine and good jobs and a great life at the end of our other moves.

My mom may have been well into her

forties, but sometimes she didn't have a clue about how the world worked.

"So when do we leave?" I asked. "And where to?"

Hannah's voice startles me, and for an instant I struggle to remember where we are.

She says, "Mandy, let's start back. My feet are getting cold."

But then she stops me. "Mandy, I wish you could see that cow over by the watering trough. Her sides are bulging so far out she must be going to have twins."

"I don't think cows do, at least not very often."

"Do you think there will be any babies soon?"

"Uncle Abe says the first calves will be born in early February."

Without warning, Hannah switches subjects. "Mandy," she says, "you've never told me about your accident. What happened?"

"Why?"

"I don't know." She sounds hurt but goes on. "I guess I've been thinking how strange it is, how I thought my life was all settled. And now my folks are probably getting divorced, and because of that one thing, all of a sudden everything else is different. Wasn't the accident like that, for you?"

I consider what she's said.

"It was and it wasn't," I finally answer. "It made everything different, but . . . there wasn't much in my life really settled before, either."

Although, I remember, I'd had hopes that things might settle down.

I remember how, for the briefest time, Mom and I had thought maybe we were going to stop being just the lonely pair that we were.

It had taken Mom several weeks and a staggering phone bill to get the name of the place that had her adoption records. But, finally, she had an agency's name and address, and it wasn't all that far north of Baltimore, where we were living.

"They said I'd have to come in person with my questions," she said.

We went up together, catching an early morning Amtrak, and by eleven we were watching a woman examine all the identification papers Mom had brought with her.

Finally the woman put them down and opened a folder.

"Actually, Karen," she said, talking to my mom, "this record of your adoption has never been sealed. Your mother left instructions to provide her name, should you ever request it."

And then she wrote several lines on a paper, which she handed, folded, to Mom. "Of course," she added, "you must understand that this address is quite old."

We were in the hall before Mom looked, her fingers trembling just a little bit, and a red spot on each cheek. I read with her, "Margaret G. McKenney," and an address in California.

Mom dithered all the way home about whether she should write or call. Then, when we got home and telephoned Information, she learned there wasn't any listing for McKenney, not at the address Mom had.

"It's a sign," Mom said. "I should write. The post office will forward a letter if she didn't move too long ago."

Mom spent three more afternoons

composing the perfect letter, finally settling on one that began, "Dear Mrs. McKenney, We have never met, but I am the daughter who . . ."

And then she wouldn't mail it until she had good stationery to copy it on to. "I want her to like me," she said.

"Mom, the kind of paper you write on won't make any difference."

"Let's go buy some," she said.

Outside, bits of dust hung in the air and a low afternoon sun glistened golden red behind them. We got into the car and Mom swung into traffic, just as a delivery truck turned a corner going too fast.

When the truck slammed into us, my seat belt kept me from being thrown through the windshield, but my head still smashed into the dashboard.

Mom had just been pulling her seat belt on when the accident happened, and she was hurled through the windshield and crushed against a utility pole.

I become aware that Hannah is waiting for me to answer and I wonder how long

I've been silent. I think back to what her question was.

"There's not much to tell," I say. "A delivery truck hit us. Mom died in the hospital several days later, and you know what happened to me."

I leave it at that. I've never really heard all the next part anyway, except that while I was starting to learn how to live without my sight, a child services worker was busy trying to figure out where to send me when I left rehab. She first tried to track down Margaret McKenney and learned she'd been dead a couple of years. Then she went to the adoption agency and from there backward to my uncles.

Sometimes I imagine the woman calling. I wonder how she asked, "Want to take in a blind teenager?"

But I suppose that's not fair. She must have worked hard to find me my family.

After Hannah goes home, Emma asks, "Want to go to the grocery store?"

When we're driving I say, "Aunt Emma, can I ask you another question?"

"Certainly."

"When you all found out about me . . . When that child services woman asked if you wanted to help . . . Did you and my uncles say yes right away, or did you have to talk it over?"

"We said yes, of course. You're family, Mandy."

"Without even talking it over?"

Aunt Emma laughs.

"I suppose we did spend an evening at the kitchen table. But the discussion started with your uncle Abe saying he'd make sure the stair railings were all safe. There was never any question what we wanted to do."

"Just because I was family?"

In a curious way I want her to say no. To tell me they wanted me for me, and not because they felt they had to take care of a relation.

Which is stupid, because how could they have wanted me for me when we'd never met?

But Aunt Emma must know what I'm thinking. She pats my leg. "Mandy," she says, "we'd want you if you didn't have a single drop of family blood."

And suddenly I feel the most awful longing for my mom, and I feel so sorry for her.

All those moves after all those things, from religion to good health . . . Maybe if she'd somehow known to move here, she'd have found what she really wanted.

I tell Aunt Emma, "I wish you'd taken my mother in."

"But Mandy," says Aunt Emma, "we didn't even know your mother existed. We never knew Gwen had a baby."

It makes me angry. "You could have known," I say. "Why didn't anybody go after Gwen?"

But I'm the one who knows the answer to that question. Abe and Gabriel were too young when Gwen left, and their mother threw Gwen's letter away.

One woman, and her meanness, spoiled Gwen's life and my mother's life.

"She could have put the envelope back together if she'd tried harder," I say.

"Who, Mandy?" asks Aunt Emma.

But I shake my head. It's too complicated.

Night comes. I open my window, pull the curtains around my shoulders, and call to Gwen.

I want to talk to Gwen, alone and signing the adoption papers that would cut her off from the last person she had a blood tie to. I want to thank her for letting me know what happened, tell her that her granddaughter is going to be OK.

A warm breeze wraps me in soft air, a breeze like the Chinook winds that blew the year Mom and I lived in Montana. I can't tell if I am wishing the words or hearing them, but a woman's voice says, "I'm glad, Mandy."

The breeze stirs, slowly lifting the lace curtains from my shoulders. They drift in front of me, hang still on the sill.

⌣ ⌣   ⌣ ⌣
⌣   ⌣
  ⌣ ⌣

chapter 16

I<small>T'S FIVE</small> more days until Christmas and I still haven't figured out gifts for Aunt Emma and my uncles. I want to be able to give them things *I've* chosen, so they'll really be gifts from *me,* but I also want to be sure the gifts are just right. Hannah has asked a couple more times if I want her help shopping, but I've told her no, I have Christmas under control. I wish.

At least I have presents for the girls at school. I take the wrapped boxes with me since it's the last day before vacation. We do our gift exchange at lunchtime.

Charla goes first, handing me a case with three colors of lip gloss. "They're all in your color family, Mandy," she says. "Just remember, the darkest is on the left and the lightest on the right."

I get a wood box with a croaking frog from Blakney, and Rosa has made ornaments for everyone. She tells me mine says, in gold glitter, ROSA AND MANDY, FRIENDS FOREVER.

And they all say they like the writing paper I give them, which has a design worked around their first names. I did it on the computer with Ted's help, which was all right to take because he's an art student and I'm not, and I printed it on parchment-feeling paper that I bought specially.

The only sad thing about our gift exchange is that Hannah is absent.

I'm surprised she didn't call to tell me she wouldn't be in school because it's not like Hannah not to call. And she didn't say a thing yesterday about not feeling well.

"A crummy time to get sick," I tell Ted as we walk to the resource room.

He *uh-huhs*, like he's not exactly agreeing, or he's thinking something else altogether.

The phone rings not long after class

starts, and a moment later Ms. Z. says the principal wants to see me.

"I'll walk Mandy over," Ted offers. "Mandy, you don't know which one the office door is, do you?" The way he asks it, I know he wants to go along.

"No," I say, "I'm not sure."

I have a sick feeling about the reason the principal has asked for me, a premonition, I guess, except . . . Well, anyway, I'm right.

"Mandy," he asks right off, "do you know where Hannah Welsh is?"

"Isn't she home sick?" I ask, hoping mostly.

"No, her father found she was gone this morning, and he's been looking and calling since." The principal's voice is stern. "Mandy, her father believes that if she's run off, she's probably gone to a friend."

"No," I say with certainty. "If Hannah went to a friend, it would be to me. And I haven't seen her."

Even as worried as I am, I'm also surprised at what I've said, at what I've realized. I am Hannah's best friend.

Ted and I go back into the hall.

"Ted," I say, keeping my voice low but

turning so he can see my mouth. "Hannah's pretty upset about her folks getting a divorce."

"I can imagine," he says. "My mother heard Hannah's mom just took off and left yesterday. For good. But that woman is such a . . . Hannah will be better off without her."

"No! That's not true." I say it so loud someone calls, "Keep it down. We're testing in here."

"Sorry," I mumble to whoever it is.

I know that Hannah was upset about her folks separating, but it would never have occurred to her that one of them might want to get away from her, too. I try to think how she'd take it. I remember the talk we had, how she'd imagined ways to run off.

"Ted, we've got to find her before she disappears forever."

"You know where she's gone?"

"I think so."

We take off right after school lets out, after first calling our folks.

Nobody's home at Ted's house or mine,

but we leave messages on the answering machines, so they won't worry.

We drive the highway in silence, except once Ted says, "That woman," and I know he's thinking about Hannah's mother.

I hear the traffic getting heavy as we get close to the city. I can feel Ted's concentration and guess he hasn't done a lot of this kind of driving. "There's a map in the glove compartment," he says.

I unfold it so that it's ready for him to look at when he gets a chance. "Turn it over," he says. "You've got it wrong side up."

"The bus station's got to be downtown," I shout. I don't want him trying to read my lips.

"We're almost there now. I'm pulling into a gas station."

And between the two of us, we get directions from a young-sounding guy who tries his hardest to act like he doesn't find anything unusual about us at all. "You're only a few blocks away," he says.

The traffic has gotten terrible, cars and trucks all around us. Once Ted jams on the brakes so hard they squeal.

There's no place to park near the depot, and I'm terrified we've arrived too late, that Hannah's already found a bus going some-place that sounds good, and that she's taken it.

"Ted, let me out, please."

He does, saying, "I'll come in as soon as I park."

Then I'm on the sidewalk, and horns are telling Ted to move on. I can't hear what he's shouting about where the depot door is.

Someone walks into my cane, knocking it clattering onto the pavement. It's put back into my hand, and a woman is saying, "Do you need help, Miss?"

And because Hannah needs help, I say, "Yes, please. Would you take me inside?"

We go through an entryway of rushing air into a station that's all echoing noise and smell, and the woman's suddenly eager not to get involved. She leaves me alone in the middle of hundreds of sounds and crowds of people.

For a moment I feel helpless, wish I'd waited for Ted. What good did I think I could do by myself? Even if Hannah's here, she can hide in my blindness.

A loudspeaker voice bounces off hard walls. ". . . to Amarillo, Albuquerque, Flagstaff, Phoenix, with connections to points south and west, now boarding in lane four."

Amarillo. *Albuquerque.* Hannah would like even the words. Flagstaff, Phoenix, they'd both sound good, too, and a desert away.

"Northbound passengers holding tickets to . . ."

That's it, I think, the loudspeaker. Maybe I can get them to put on an announcement for Hannah, say, "Will passenger Hannah Welsh please check in at the counter?"

But first I've got to find it myself.

I walk forward until my cane runs into someone's foot. "Please," I say, "would you show me which way the ticket counters are?"

Someone pushes from behind, and whoever I've asked doesn't answer.

I bump into a child. Hear a slap, a woman saying, "Can't you see she's blind?"

The noise is louder to my left, and I think

that perhaps the counters are that way. I turn, run my cane out but not up, and bang my face into cold metal.

The loudspeaker blares again, "Final call for passengers to Albuquerque, Flagstaff, Phoenix." Its twanging threat echoes through the depot.

Is Hannah outside, waiting to board? Maybe already sitting on the bus?

I have to get to the counter, get someone to look for her quickly.

"Please," I say to whoever can hear. "Would someone please . . ."

Kids start laughing, and a girl says, "She shouldn't be alone."

I bump into another person, a woman who says, "The back of the line's over there." Her voice is bored and thinly hostile.

"This is an emergency," I tell her. "Would you . . ."

She doesn't let me finish. "Why do you people think you shouldn't have to wait in line like the rest of us?"

The panic I've been fighting to hold in starts to well up.

"Hannah," I call out, "Hannah?"

The loudspeaker crackles, blares out, "First call for passengers to Oklahoma City, Tulsa, Springfield, St. Louis. Your bus is now ready for boarding in lane four."

Lane four . . . That means the Albuquerque bus has left. Please, please, don't let Hannah be on it.

Whatever is inside me, despair and frustration, anger, raw screaming panic, it boils up and takes over. "HanNAH!" I shout as loudly as I can, loud, pulling every bit of air from my lungs, "HANNAHHHHHHHHH!" loud, and everyone, everything silences around me.

Silences all for one brief stretching-out-to-forever moment, and I think every person in that depot is holding his breath. Then a titter sweeps around me, a relieved whisper that lets people get on with talking and waiting and saying good-bye to each other, a rising wave of sound that lets them pretend I'm not there.

chapter 17

 ɔ ɔ ɔ ɔ
 ɔ ɔ ɔ ɔ
   ɔ ɔ

ALL I'VE DONE is make a fool of myself.

Someone grabs my arm and I flinch. Who would grab so hard?

Close by my face a voice demands, "What are you doing here?" A voice so angry, so harsh, I almost don't recognize it as Hannah's. "Why did you come?"

"To get you, Hannah," I say. "Ted and I want to take you home."

"I don't have a home." Hannah's words hit hot against my cheek, a tiny fleck of spittle wets my neck. "I don't need your help. Why don't you mind your own business and leave me alone?"

"Why didn't you?" I'm suddenly as furious as she is. "You didn't have to come over, help the blind girl, just because I shouted."

"What, I should have just left you?" she says. "I couldn't."

"Well, I couldn't either."

Then the ridiculousness of it reaches us both, how we're mad at each other for doing the same thing. It doesn't make things right, but it's enough that we can talk.

When Ted finds us we're sitting together on a bench, and I'm telling Hannah how afraid I was she'd caught that bus to Albuquerque.

"It was full," she says. "But I'm going to take the next one, to there or anyplace else where I won't ever have to see Texas or my so-called family again."

"How are you going to live?" Ted asks, like he's really curious. Like Hannah going off somewhere to live on her own is even an option.

"Look, I'll be all right." Hannah's words are thick and I think her throat must ache with the strain of not crying. She blows her nose. I imagine her sitting up, straightening her spine. "I got a cash advance on my dad's charge card that I'll pay back. Enough to hold me until I find a job."

"Doing what?" Ted asks. "Working in a fast-food place?"

But they've both lost the point. "Hannah," I say, "you do have a home."

"No. I'm not wanted."

I'd like to tell her, "Of course you are," but I realize that if I'm not honest, she won't listen.

So I say, "Hannah, you don't know if your mother wants you or not. Her going . . . It might not have anything to do with you. I mean, she left your whole family."

I think of Gwen's mother, tearing up Gwen's letter and then trying to piece the envelope back together.

"Hannah, she may not even know herself what she wants, or who."

"But she's my *mother*." Hannah makes it both a plea and a question, and I don't have an answer.

So instead I say, "How about your father and brother? You know they want you."

"They'll get along."

Maybe, I think. And maybe not. Maybe her brother needs her as much as Abe needed Gwen. I'm trying to think how to explain that when I realize what it is that I really have to say.

"Hannah, I want you to come back. You're my best friend."

She waits, and I know I must say the rest of it. "And you're the first best friend I've ever had. I need you."

There's this horrible long moment that she doesn't answer. I feel like I'm standing naked in the middle of a million staring strangers, all pointing and saying, "She's never had a friend."

And then Hannah makes everything right. She says, "Best *girl* friend. Remember, Ted's the sensitive type."

We drive away from the city, all three of us jammed in the front seat, me in the middle.

I think, I'm the one who's holding us together.

Ted's whistling "The Eyes of Texas," and I wonder what he hears in his head, and if he knows he is perfectly on key.

Then, when we're almost home and Ted has shifted to Christmas music and is way

down in the low notes of "We Three Kings,"
I get an idea.

"Ted, can we stop by the mall?"

"Never be able to park," he says, but he
takes us there anyway, and after driving
around for a while, we get a space.

"Let's call your dad, Hannah," I say. "And
then . . . I need to buy presents. Especially
for Aunt Emma. Will you help?"

Christmas morning I wake to a springlike
breeze coming in my window. I go over,
lean out, listen to the voices of my uncles
calling to each other and to the cattle
they're feeding. Gabriel must see me, because he calls up, "Merry Christmas,
Mandy."

I pick up my mother's picture, imagine a
face more soft than I used to see it, and
with the beginnings of peace in her eyes.

I run my finger down the airman's picture. Maybe his grin is for me, too.

And then I'm washed and dressed and
downstairs, and Aunt Emma and the uncles
are squabbling about whether we do presents or have breakfast first.

"May as well get ready to starve, Abe,"

Uncle Gabriel says. "Emma's no more patient than a kid."

Only it's Uncle Gabriel who has made a small carpet-covered jungle gym that he can't wait for me to open.

"What's it for?" I ask, and he puts a kitten in my arms.

It's a little bigger than my opossum was the last time he scrambled up the porch steps to me. He didn't stay even for a whole bottle that time, and it made me realize he had stopped needing me. That he'd learned how to live on his own.

But this kitten—oh, I can love this kitten even when it's all grown up. I snuggle it close while it explores with tiny paws to find out who I am.

Then my aunt and uncles are telling me to circle the tree and feel all the other presents under it. "All the velvet bows, those are all for you," Aunt Emma says. "Open one."

But I rub my face in the kitten's fur. I make my voice stay steady because this is a dumb time to get weepy. I say, "It's your turn now."

I want them to like their gifts. Want so much that I ache.

Uncle Abe goes first. I've made him a tiny circus of toothpicks tipped with colored flags, planted in a surface of plaster of paris textured with dust. Little plastic people sit on a ring of pebbles, watching pill bugs climb a slide. Ted made the pill bugs for me out of clay, after pointing out they weren't really bugs at all but a land-living crustacean called an isopod. Right.

Emma and Gabriel don't know what to make of the circus, and for a while I'm afraid Abe doesn't, either. Then he says, "If you can get a message through to Gwen, tell her thanks for remembering."

Gabriel whispers, "What's all that about?"

Emma shushes him.

Then Gabriel opens his gift, a combination knife and screwdriver. "See," I tell him. "It's got two sizes each of Phillips and slot, and three blades and . . ."

"And just what I need," he says. "I'm going to keep it right where I can always get at it."

And then Aunt Emma is lifting tissue paper from the sweater I've bought her. "It's for your pleated skirt," I say. "The new one from the mall."

"I'm wearing it," Aunt Emma says. "Mandy, the color match couldn't be more perfect."

"Hannah helped me. I asked her."

And I give Aunt Emma a big hug. Her cheek is wet against mine.

"Don't cry," I say. "Merry Christmas. I love you."

chapter 18

S PRING has come, and I leave my window open to it all the time. Open to the wind that blows almost constantly, that Emma tells me I'll wish for, once summer gets here.

Ask me what has changed and I'll tell you.

I'll say how the figure that cartwheeled from the sky lies still and rests now. I think of him and the others in graves beneath budding trees, under yellow sun and blue sky and red tulips.

I especially imagine a lot of red tulips about my mother's grave because she liked to respect her contrasts.

Aunt Emma and the uncles act younger than they did when I first came here, even though Gabriel says I'm giving him more gray hair every day. "Mandy," he tells me, "you think of stuff to do faster than I can think of rules for keeping you safe doing it."

But his only real rule is that I don't worry Aunt Emma.

The opossum doesn't come back anymore, but thanks to Uncle Abe I'm still in the stepmothering business, taking care of an orphaned calf now. Abe named her for me, Mandy Girl, because she was born on my sixteenth birthday. I give her milk from a huge bottle, and one of these days she's probably going to get tired of my kitten trying to get in on the feeding.

And Abe likes to talk with me about Gwen. He's remembering more and more about being a boy, more than his pill bug circus.

Yes, ask me what has changed and I'll tell you.

I have.

I can't pretend everything is OK. I can't see, and in some ways I'm just now beginning to realize how huge that loss is. Maybe it took getting past being angry to know.

And to realize how much more I have to learn.

I'm going away for eight weeks this summer, to live in a dorm with other blind kids and work in a day care center. My caseworker helped set it up, and Mr. Burkhart wrote me a great letter of recommendation. It has me scared, both the job and how I'll get along in the dorm, but I keep telling myself the Great Om wouldn't send me off to something I can't handle.

Hannah and Ted have both promised to visit.

The town I'll be in is just a couple of miles from where Mrs. Welsh is living now, and I think maybe Hannah might try to see her, too.

And Ted's been saving money so he'll be able to call often. He's got this special phone that puts the volume high enough that he can usually hear what's said.

And some things are better than they ever have been, maybe the more important things.

Uncle Gabriel says every person's life has a time when he lives the fullest, the most aware. The army was like that for him, he says, the time he goes back to and longs for, with all its good and bad.

Aunt Emma says nonsense, and she can think of lots of years when she's been quite fully alive, thank you. No one tells her how her voice softens and yearns when she talks about the few months she and Uncle Gabriel lived in Mexico, when she was expecting the baby that died.

So I wonder. I hope my time is still out in front of me, that it will be more spectacular, bigger, than it is now, but . . . I don't know. Right now I feel more alive than I ever have.

No, that's not exactly it.

Right now the world feels more alive to me than it ever has, a world for me to reach out to and touch.

And I've changed in one more way.

I've made room for Gwen inside me, and for my mom, and maybe even for Gwen's mother. I know how to feel, and love, for us all.